WRAPPED

IN

SAPPHIRE

An Erotic Office Romance Novel

Nora S. Pattugalan

Book design by Nora S. Pattugalan

Published by Nora S. Pattugalan

ISBN: 979-8-9889402-2-7

https://norapauthor.com/

For those tempted by love and its surprises.

1

Edith steps out of the car, clicking her heels on the pavement. Leaves blew in the wind, swaying by her as she crossed the street. Pedestrians stare as she hustles to the building without a sweat. More cold air slaps against her cheeks as she walks into the building. Harry on her left looked at her, lifting an eight-ounce cup. Edith smiles, taking the cup and feeling the heat transfer to her hand. He had already whipped up her usual favorite; Brazilian coffee with cinnamon creamer and whip.

"Thanks, Harry. You're the best." she nearly whispers.

"No problem, Edith. Have a nice day," he waves goodbye. Edith remembered the call about an abrupt seven o'clock meeting.

She sips the drink carefully, using her free hand to untangle the knots in her hair. Her auburn curls bounce. Edith's lipstick smears as she drinks from the cup. Groaning, she started combing her hair with her fingers. She paced to a wall mirror nearby.

She pulls out her crimson red Yves Saint Laurent lipstick and smears it across her lips, smacking them to even out the color.

"Reginald is going to kill me if I'm late," she mutters.

Everyone around her stood speaking loudly. The marble floors reflected a woman's ankles and heels. An older gentleman walked over to another and shook his hand.

The coffee he was holding nearly spilled. Edith looked away and groaned at her tardiness.

She worked for nearly six years at this company and no one acknowledged her efforts in ordering people from the engineering team. She was their boss, their coordinator, but there were other things Edith hoped to do besides sit at her desk and write reports. Sometimes, she would make phone calls and leave messages for Reginald or his assistant, but the upper management warned her not to ask any more questions as they expected her to know what to do. They wanted her to download knowledge and present ideas.

Standing impatiently, Edith tapped her foot and rummaged through her purse for her phone. To the left of the lobby was a man she's never seen before sitting in the fabric arm chair. He lowered the magazine in his hands and watched Edith intently. The stranger leaned forward to lift his mug from the coffee table. He crossed his leg over the other.

Edith glances over her shoulder, noting his gaze. *It's too early for this.* She shifts her eyes at the elevator to her right, then looked around before walking up to the doors. *What is he looking at?* A short smirk crept on his face, making shivers go down her spine. She pressed the elevator button and puffed air out of her cheeks. *Come on, I'm late.*

She watched as people entered and exited the building. Several men had suitcases in their hands. In the lobby, an older man greeted a young woman, congratulating her on receiving an award last week. Edith sighed, wishing she gained recognition for something. The fourth quarter of the year had just begun and Edith was hoping for a job upgrade so she could afford to move out of her rusty old house.

Being one of the best coders of the company, they could at least move her up to the next level in her career or add a pay raise. She would do anything to make more money except quit and search for another job.

This conference was supposed to be a big deal. It meant abrupt meetings were urgent for a company like this. Was there a new project announcement? Did they hire new recruits to be trained? Edith was hoping for the promotion as she was nearing her six-year mark. Before leaving the company, Dan Foster wasn't the greatest boss she's had, but he acknowledged her efforts at pitch meetings; that's at least once a month.

Dan praised Edith for the smallest things. It was sad to see him go, but he moved on to better things. She learned to be happy about his endeavors.

Edith directed her eyes at the elevator light. A minute passed, and it still hadn't lit up.

A shadow moved behind Edith, making her look behind her right shoulder. The cologne fragrance was of cedar and lemon. She cleared her throat and tapped on her thigh. Her pencil skirt pressed against her skin.

"I can't believe the elevator is slow again." A voice spoke.

Despite a devilish grin, he's calm, trying to make a joke out of the situation. Edith smiles uncomfortably, glancing over her shoulder at him. Can this elevator open already? She pressed the button again.

Come on, please. As she wished, the bell dings and the doors open. The man, now behind her, gestures for Edith to enter first. She pressed her lips and took a step forward, then pressed the button for the third floor. The man excused himself and pressed for the second floor. He stood tall with his hands clasped in front of him.

He then looked down at Edith's bright red pumps. She was too busy in her thoughts, contemplating about a bigger paycheck, twirling her fingers into her wavy red strands. His eyes scanned up her legs, noting her smooth bare skin and black pencil skirt. Edith licked her lips, not worrying about his wandering eyes.

Edith rubbed her eye, and an eyelash fell out. She noticed him taking a quick look at her backside. He leans to his right and puts his hand gently on her ass cheek. He pressed his palm against her and a low groan vibrates through his throat. Edith's eyes flashed to her left, and he clears his throat and stands still, almost locking his knees.

His hand was warm and caused Edith's skin to grow warmer. She glanced at the sly smirk on his face. No man has touched Edith in over three years.

Slight pressure pulsed in her pussy. Not now. The elevator dings, and he removes his hand. The doors open to the second floor.

She straightened her back and shifted her feet, hoping to shake off the stranger.

The elevator bell dings just in time.

"This is my stop," he groaned.

Edith sighed. What the fuck happened? That was weird. Her cheeks turned scarlet, remembering that the stranger had touched her. She could report to the HR, but how would she explain the light dampness in her panties? The elevator stops at the third floor and Edith shakes off the thought. The lights on this floor flicked above her. There was a visible crack in the ceiling. Edith clicked her tongue and wondered if the maintenance guy was around.

She took a breath and walked past the empty cubicles, turning to her right for the first conference room. No one was inside. One light was on, but everywhere else on this floor was dark, except for a floor lamp at the end of the hall. Surely, they must have known what time the meeting started. Edith looked up at the wall clock. 6:45 AM. She sat down in the fourth seat near the door and put her purse on her lap.

Before doing anything else, she pulled the phone out of her purse to check emails.

Edith clicked on the message which read BRIGHTON TECH conference at 7 AM. Don't be late. The irony set in because everyone was late. If there was a rescheduling, she would know. Her bladder notified her at the wrong time. Edith stood up from the seat and clutched onto her purse. The closest restroom was down the hall.

She walked down the hall in a rush. She turned to her right and opened the women's restroom door. "At least the restroom is unlocked." she muttered.

Time moved quickly. When she finished, Edith made her way back to the conference room. Towards the back of the floor, the lights were partially on. Someone must have arrived early to work on something. She smiles at the determination this person had. From down the hall, more lights were lit up and Edith's heart raced. *I'm ready. Let's get this meeting over with.*

The shadow of a man stepped into the light. "Finally!" she sighed. "That must be the boss." her stomach churned in excitement. She swallowed.

She made it around the corner when a heavy weight turned her onto her back and a hand covered her mouth. A familiar scent made itself known to her. Edith squealed and groaned. Her eyes blinked at the darkness. She looked to the right, seeing if anyone could help her.

"Not so fast." the scarcely enticing stranger grabbed her hands and pinned Edith against the wall.

His other hand pressed on her mouth, preventing her from screaming. *This is it. I'm going to lose my job today. Goodbye, promotion.* The sounds she made muffled through his fingers. He placed her palm on his hardening cock. Edith's own arousal increased. *Oh, fuck.* She moved her feet, trying to free herself. She could step on his foot and ruin his shiny loafers. Edith groans. The heat of from his hard-on sent tingles near her slit. She could bite his finger, but the stranger's other hand kept her distracted.

His scent hovered over her face. Her eyes widened. He was the man in the elevator. He towers over her, keeping her body steady.

"You're that tease from the fifth floor, aren't you? I've heard about you little minx." his voice was low and intense.

"I'm already late,"

"You're late, you say? That won't be a problem. You seem so stressed this morning. Why don't we have a little fun?" he frees the hand from her mouth and tears her blouse open with both hands, exposing Edith's bare breasts. "My, my." he leans down and sucks the right nipple. His lips could burn her skin. She moaned.

He looked up at her and circles his tongue around the hardened point. Is this really happening? She relaxed. She can't stop him now. A sly grin spread across his face. He drops his hands and holds onto her hips. The stranger flicked his tongue on one nipple, moving over to the other, sending electric pleasure throughout her body.

His right hand moved up her thigh and hiked up her skirt carefully. Edith swallowed and inhaled nervously. His hand met with her warm mound and he cups it.

He twisted his fingers on her right nipple. "This won't take long, but I want to play." he growls, rubbing his hand on her slit. Her panties soak again. "I recognize you now. You're that little slut from the fifth floor, aren't you?" his voice was as rough as his grip. Where is everyone? Between breaths, Edith could hear the clock on the wall ticking, making her temperature rise higher.

It appears his scent grew stronger, making Edith clench her thighs together. He smiles and reached into her panties, then circled his thumb on her clitoris. I'm weak. Her moan prompted him to stop and rest his hand on her pubes.

"Answer me," he says, looking into her eyes.

"Yes," she swallowed.

She never wanted a stranger this badly. Correction, they wanted each other. Edith wanted for someone to touch her.

"Yes?"

She gasped as his hand reached down to her clitoris again. He moved his thumb faster in a clockwise motion, pressing harder.

"Yes, I am!" she pants.

Edith couldn't take it anymore. This man is so hot, but how could he want me? Her secretion dripped onto his fingers. His cologne latched onto her clothes. The smell of cedar, lemon, and cum mixed to fill her nostrils with ecstasy. The stranger pulled his hand out of her panties and smirked.

"So, tell me. Do you have a boyfriend?" he asked, examining his hand.

"No," she paused. Edith's heart was nearly down in the pit of her stomach. "No, I don't have a boyfriend," her eyes rose to meet his.

"Hmm," This was all he could say, pressing down the wrinkles on his shirt and pulling at his silk midnight blue tie.

His casual demeanor transitions back. Edith watched as he tucked his hands into the pockets of his black slacks and leaned his back against the wall. How could he act as if nothing happened?

2

The man was at least four inches taller than Edith. His dark chocolate hair and hazel eyes called to her. Since he stopped fondling her, Edith's cheeks cooled down, and she picked her purse off the floor. Her eyes widened as realization struck her.

I should walk back to the conference room now. She twirled a strand of hair and walked forward.

"If you'll excuse me, I have to go."

His mouth opened to speak. She took a quick look at the man and bowed her head. Edith tugged onto her skirt and patted down the wrinkles. She shrugged at the buttons, leaving the top two undone. The touch of his hand against her thighs lingered in her mind. She glanced back, and he waved at her, smiling.

"What a strange guy," Edith exhaled deeply. Her clitoris pulses, and another drip falls into her panties. The aching pain of wanting more spins in her head, causing her pussy to tingle.

He was tall, dark, and handsome. The image of a man she had only seen in movies. Her mind lingered on the trace of his shaped abs and the smoothness of his skin.

Not a minute passed, and she turned around. "Oh," she moaned. "Fuck the meeting," she breathed, turning back around. She walked back to the man, who turned around just in time to see her approaching him. She looked straight into his eyes.

There were two outcomes from her actions. One, she would have this man take her and there would be no consequences afterwards, and two, they would get caught and upper management would chew them out. She didn't even know this man and here she was, desiring him. They equally jeopardized her dreams of a promotion.

Edith walked faster towards him without a second thought. The man's eyes grew bigger as she flung her arms around his neck and reached up for those lips of his. *God, they're soft.*

She smiles at herself, pressing her body against this emperor of a man. He breathes and turns to Edith, pinning her back against the wall again. He returned a soft kiss and ensured his crotch was meeting hers.

"You smell delectable, do you want me as much as I want you?" he whispers between each kiss. Edith pressed herself against him, moving her hips to tease him.

"We have little time," she said. He allowed her to breathe and ran his hands up her sides.

"What?" he gazed into her eyes, curving his eyebrows. Wasn't he the one in control?

"Take me." she breathed. Edith's tempting aura pulls his body closer to hers.

"You really are a slut."

He paused and stepped over to the corner for the light switch.

The entire floor goes dark and Edith looked down to her right. No one was at the back cubicle after all. It was foolish to be in the complete dark with a stranger, but her gut urged her to trust him now.

Edith locked her eyes with his, and a chill ran down her spine.

"I'll guide you." He took her hand and hesitated. "Have you been fucked before?" The man took her hand and pulled her in, holding her close as if she was being saved from a fall.

It was too late. She was already falling for him. Flustered, she wanted to push him away but her arms went numb.

"I've fucked a few times before." Edith batted her eyes innocently and relaxed herself in his arms.

Her two previous boyfriends weren't as possessive as this man. His impulse excited Edith. She looked down at the hem of her skirt, wanting his hand to be up her thighs. What if this was too much?

What if he didn't want her anymore? The man looked at her for a minute longer.

"Is something wrong?" she asked.

He pulled her to an empty desk and bent her over. She gasped and giggled, feeling the thrill of the rush. Edith glances back at him as he pressed his groin against her ass. His cock hardens at an instant.

"I'll show you I'm better than those who fucked you."

Edith groaned and gulped. She gently placed her hands on either side of her and lifted her head, waited for the push. Edith's pussy moistens from the anticipation. She cleared her throat as he rubbed against her more. Oh, please. Edith closed her eyes and breathed. Finally, he pulled her skirt and her panties followed. He smiles at the cum stain.

The man swept her hair over her shoulder and stroked his cock, preparing it for the beginning push. He licked his shivering fingers and rubbed Edith's slit. His shaky breath transferred, causing Edith's heart to race. The head of his cock met with her opening and she pressed her lips, feeling his tip.

Without warning, his cock pushes through her opening, thrusting slowly. The man groans and she feels the outline of his abs as he leaned into her with each thrust. He breathes and shows off with a quick thrust, surprising Edith. Her cheeks turn red and she let out a low moan. She whimpered and moaned with each careful thrust.

"How's this? You're so wet for me."

He picked up the pace and thrusted faster, harder. Edith's heart was going to burst. She breathed hard through her nostrils and gasped for air. Her arms spread out on the desk as he plummeted his cock harder and faster. The office floor was quiet, but the sound of oozing cum and his balls slapping against her ass filled the air.

This was quite comical to him. No one was at the office yet. Edith wondered why as she was being drilled, but she didn't care anymore. She was in heaven. He pulled out, then entered forcefully. Edith moaned loud enough that it echoes down two rows of cubicles. She squealed and moan, exciting her play mate. He gripped onto her hips and thrusted harder, quicker.

The items on the desk shook, and some things rolled off the desk from this mini earthquake. He shook her weight, moaning and groaning along with her. In the middle of this, the man unbuttoned the top of his dress shirt to cool down his slightly darker skin. Seeing the outline of his pectorals made Edith push herself up against him. She was in the happiest state she's ever been this week. The thought of a morning fuck session with a man she may never see again made her explode more.

"My slut is so wet." he whispered into her right ear.

He cupped her breasts and ripped her blouse open. My slut? Edith thought. I like that. She moaned in response and he pulled out again. "I want more," she moaned.

Her heart slid down as she thought the fun was over. He pinched her nipples with both hands, keeping her bent over. He kept her shirt wide open, brushing his hands on her skin. Edith's knees shivered and bent while his fingers explored her breasts. He smiles to himself and put his lips to her ear. "Patience, pet."

He pushed onto her back, making her breasts press onto the table. The icy surface hardened her nipples further. He stroked her hair, and the movement tickled her neck. She eased her posture. "Please," she whimpered.

Two fingers shoved inside her pussy and Edith adjusted to feel his fingers wiggle inside her. He pumped his fingers vigorously, making her scream. I can't believe this is happening.

"Enjoying yourself, little minx?" he slowed the pace and felt her folds dry up, her pussy clutched onto his fingers. He breathed into her ear, inhaling her scent slowly. "That's enough foreplay."

She couldn't get enough. Edith felt selfish, so greedy that he was the only man she'd allow to devour her. His pet names for her made Edith want more of him. She needed him as her oxygen.

He stuck his cock inside her, smiling at the sound.

Edith made the first move, bucking her hips. He gently rocked her and helped her move at his rhythm. She was eagerly wanting to melt on his hard-on.

He noticed her increased desire for him and pumped faster, showing no mercy.

"Oh my God," Edith moans.

Her lips dried and chapped.

His pre-cum trickles down and spills out of the tip. Edith moans and curses, feeling his balls slap against her again. With four hard thrusts, he shot his load inside.

"Shit. That wasn't supposed—"

"That was perfect."

3

Edith sat at her desk. She taps her pen and bit her lip, trying to conduct the perfect email while keeping her notes app open for new ideas for the engineers to build on. She opened her planner and flipped the page to look for the date. That's odd. She could have sworn she jotted down the now skipped meeting for the seventeenth of this month. The only thing she found was her sloppy handwriting that read Costume party for the thirtieth.

She looked through the glass wall and groaned at the orange and black décor. Halloween was her favorite holiday and autumn was her favorite season. Edith wasn't thrilled to have mess all over the fifth floor. Were these skeleton decorations necessary? Someone passed by Edith's office and twisted the doorknob.

Bianca entered with a grin on her face and a basket of chocolate in her hand. "Happy almost Halloween, Edith!" she placed a couple of chocolate candy bars on the right side of the desk. Edith looked at her computer screen and down at the chocolate. Bianca's lips curved. "Aren't you excited?"

"I am excited. I just have so much work to do this week." she scratched her forehead and bit her tongue.

"Well, you have four more days until you can finally relax. Let's have some fun. Come to the costume party with me."

"I suppose you're right." Edith folded her hands. "Hey, did you hear anything back about a meeting we were supposed to have last week?" she licked her lips.

Voices filled Edith's mind. Her own moans and whispers coming from her mystery man's mouth filled her ears. His dirty words floated in and out of her mind, and Edith was completely out of the zone.

Bianca curved her eyebrows and darted her eyes to think. "Was there supposed to be a meeting? I don't believe I heard anything about a meeting."

"Huh. Are you sure?" Edith scooted her chair closer to listen.

"Perhaps, there was a conference call or something for the other engineers. I haven't attended a formal meeting since last quarter. I can't recall." Bianca held onto the basket handle as she faced away from Edith.

"Thanks, Bianca." Edith said, continuing to type on the keyboard.

Bianca looked at Edith. "Of course, Edith. Enjoy your chocolate." she turned the handle. "I'll see you at the party."

Edith nods with a smile. She logged into her email and scrolled down her inbox. There was no way a meeting would go unnoticed. The message was from the Brighton corporation to Brighton Tech and Associates.

Edith ran her hands over her face. There's a message, it's not like it doesn't exist.

Attention Brighton Associates,

There will be a meeting in the main conference room on the third floor. Please keep in mind that the Chief Executive Officer will be in the building for this meeting. The event will begin at seven o'clock and end at eight. Please be timely and presentable.

Thank you, Brighton Technologies.

Was it a hoax? She stared at the computer, her eyes dried and turned red. If she were smart, she'd check the CC label. Edith might have missed the largest conference of the year just to be fucked by a man she hardly knew.

She rubbed her temples. "This is all a dream and it'll go away. Goodbye, promotion." she groaned. Why do you have to be such a horny slut, Edith?

The day had gone by slowly. By five in the afternoon, most of the employees called it a day and went home. Four people were on the office floor, chatting and typing away. Edith grinned at how motivated people can be to finish their jobs. While she was their lead coder, the manager of all coders on this floor, Edith felt like she never caught a break. She clicked her mouse and typed the last paragraph for her notes.

Four engineers emailed her last night, wanting clarification and suggestions on what customers might like. She stared at her device prototypes.

Edith sighed and put her elbow on her desk. She logged out of the computer and stared at the bright baby blue wall in her office. Next to the door was an end table with a lamp on top. In Edith's office was a mini bookshelf that comprised engineering how-to books and textbooks. None of this meant she wasn't knowledgeable.

She wanted to pull out a textbook but her brain was exhausted.

Edith thought of another idea. Not wanting to go home just yet, she got up from her chair and pulled the blinds down to cover her windows. Nobody from the office floor could see what she was planning. She turned and pulled the blinds to shield herself from the outside. The room was now dim, aside from the lamplight. Edith stared at the beanbag chair to her left. Great idea. She slipped the heels off her feet and pulled the desk drawer.

In her hand was a purple eight-inch dildo. She needed to relieve herself again somehow. Men on this floor wouldn't dare to touch her. In the room's corner, Edith takes the dildo and sinks herself into the green beanbag chair. Her ass sinks in as she spread her legs. She opened her legs and pulled up the skirt of her dress, revealing her smooth pink pussy lips. It was amazing how her juices didn't drip down despite not wearing panties today.

This is so filthy; she thought. If it were truly obscene, then why would she keep a sex toy in her office drawer?

She pictured the tall, suited, handsome stranger who she fucked days before. Where could her mystery man be? She rubbed the toy in between her folds, wishing it was his cock. Edith stuck the toy inside her and gasped. If no one heard that, then the walls must have been sound proof.

She continued to push the dildo all the way in, controlling it with her right hand so the movement was slow. Her pussy ejected a low squirt. White milky liquid splashed out from a tiny spurt. She moved faster, picturing her mystery man towering over her in this bean bag. Was it uncomfortable? Yes. Her back leaned just fine, but Edith's neck was throwing a fit. She breathed through her nostrils carefully and moaned quietly, pumping the rubber cock in and out.

More spurts of cum came out, possibly staining her dress. She didn't care about that right now. There was a pack of baby wipes somewhere in this room. Edith moved faster, hearing the man's words echo in her head. She closed her eyes. His voice rings in her ears. "Cum for me, little minx." he says, licking his lips in her mind, and moves closer for a kiss. Yearning for his lips, she pumps the dildo quicker. Her wrist ached from the sudden movements.

"Oh, take me. Please!" she moaned while covering her mouth with the other hand. "Mmm!" her orgasm was uncontrollable. Her moans wanted to take over. Edith breathed and groaned as she worked the toy, believing that it moved on its own. "Yesss!" she whispered through her teeth. A final release of cum splashed onto her hand, and her eyes rolled back slightly.

Her pussy pulsed, ejecting the remaining pumps. Two knocks on the door made Edith shut her legs instinctively.

"Ms. Rosu, is everything alright?"

"Yes! Everything is fine," she breathed.

"I'll be going now, Ms. Rosu." The woman said. Yes, please leave.

"Alright, Sonya, I'll see you tomorrow."

Edith looked down at the mess she made and snickered. The dildo was still inside her dripping pussy, but she felt her muscles ache.

Chairs were being pushed in and footsteps moved down the hall. She could hear the elevator ding and voices faded.

"Great. Now that I'm completely spent, you all left." she muttered. She looked at the toy and pumped the thing a few times, feeling her dry lips moisten again. "Ahh, I have to stop."

Edith got a hold of herself and pulled the toy out. She smiles at how naughty and flushed she was. Edith grabbed the baby wipes from her lower desk drawer and wiped the toy clean before wrapping it into a clean napkin and putting it back into the main drawer.

"All work and no play? I don't think so," she whispered before switching off the lamp light.

She turned, clicked around to shut down her computer, grabbed her purse, and stepped out. Edith closed the door behind her and locked it before walking to the elevator.

The next morning, the second tier engineer knocked on Edith's office door. He tapped his right foot, waiting patiently for her to open it. Edith was sitting at her desk with a pen in her mouth and her hand on the computer mouse.

Edith stood up from the desk and put her notebook to the side. "Just give me a second, please," she clicked away.

She was busily browsing the company website, seeing if she could scour the directory for her mystery man. Where are you? Edith took the pen out of her mouth and put it back into the holder. She pressed her hands down her blouse to flatten the wrinkles and casually opened the door.

"Albert," she lowered her eyes as her heels made him seem an inch shorter than he was. "What can I help you with?"

"Ms. Rosu, everyone should have received a notification for a post-lunch meeting. I just thought you should know." he smirked. His British accent flowed through. An actual meeting; she thought. I won't be late this time.

She walked over to the end table and pulled out the drawer. She found her mini makeup bag and a dusty compact mirror. Edith sighed in relief and walked back to her desk. Thoughts of her mystery man lingered again.

She sat in her office chair and leaned back. Will he be at the meeting? Maybe I'll find out who he is.

Rescheduling meetings wasn't unusual for the company to do, but missing a meeting to fuck was something they can never find out about. Edith smiles to herself, but a pinch of guilt met with her gut. She felt eighteen with a crush; a proscriptive and naughty crush who can make her cum.

4

Perhaps, Edith got the dates mixed up. The following day, everybody rushed to the conference room on the second floor. I'm a fucking idiot; Edith cursed. Not wanting to seem aloof, she followed her peers down the hall and into the room. The whiteboard was blank and there was no sign on the door.

Edith looked at Bianca then dropped her gaze. You're the manager. You should know about these things. Edith puffed air out of her cheeks and waited for everyone to sit before making her way to a chair. Bianca tapped her pen on the table. She placed her purse on her lap and took out a mini Snickers bar. Edith pulled the chair on Bianca's left and Albert sat across from her. Bianca grinned and asked Albert if he wanted a chocolate bar.

He chuckled nervously and said, "I'll pass." then leaned forward to speak to Edith. "Hey, do you know who the moderator is today?"

Edith shrugged. "I thought you knew."

He smiles and shrugged. Edith looked down at her nails, not wanting to seem clueless. Although she was the manager, she still wasn't up-to-date with last-minute meetings. She was very much clueless when bad luck struck.

This may mark a strike on her promotion status. Four more people from the engineering team, one intern, and two leads, entered the conference room. Edith thought of when she was supposed to be in this room days ago. The chair wheels skid on the carpet and cushions squeaked. Edith stared at the drink coaster in front of her.

"Alright! Who's ready for a meeting?" A familiar face walked into the room. Edith's hands shivered, making her drop the coaster. Her eyes widened as it fell to the floor, rolling shortly.

The man met her eyes. His smile was warm, comforting. It boosted everyone's enthusiasm; causing Edith to snap out of her trance and contain herself. To Edith, his charming grin was admittedly arousing. Her eyes locked with his and he stood in front of the white board.

She cleared her throat and bowed her head as he passed by. His irritating cologne pulled her in once again. She cursed under her breath and squirmed. Clearing her throat, she turned to Bianca. "I'll be right back. I need some water." Bianca nodded as Edith stood, turning away from the walking cologne bottle.

"Sit down, Ms. Rosu." the man slithered the letter S in Rosu. Cold sweat rolled down Edith's neck. Her eyes widened as she turned and sank back into the seat. How did you know my name?

He pointed at a chair closer to him now. Bianca smiles at the space between. Edith looked at her in horror, then back at the man staring at her with his brooding eyes. This has to be a prank. I'm being set up.

He looked back at the group and straightens his posture. "I apologize for canceling the meeting on short notice. There was," he paused, glancing at Edith. "an emergency."

Albert looked at Edith with a smirk. A low chuckle rolled up his throat, then he choked. His cough echoed, adding to the discomfort in this room. Do men have telepathy? Edith thought, shooting Albert a look.

The man adjusted his tie and wrote letters on the board. Felix Radley. Edith looked at the name and raised her eyebrows curiously. She's never met a Felix Radley before. He must be a new hire, or perhaps he's the vice president's son. He looked rather young, possibly thirty-five. Edith has passed by elderly men in this building plenty of times. At twenty-eight, Edith was respected by everyone.

She stared at the table, thinking hard enough about who this guy might be.

He looked straight at her and then looked around speaking to everyone else. "I know what you might be thinking. Who the hell is this guy?" he laughs to himself.

There was a giggle coming from the right side of the table and two more people joined in with their dry laughs. He turned and took the dry-erase marker and wrote again. Edith looked over at the others and was feeling as if she was attending her first day of school. Felix wrote three letters under his name.

CEO? That can't be true. Edith opens her lips, nearly catching air in her throat. The veins in her wrists twitched. *Great job, Edith. You've fucked your way to the top.*

"I might not be familiar to some of you, but I am the Chief Executive Officer and owner of this company." he cleared his throat. "This is your first annual meeting with me." he released a quick laugh. "It's going to be fun, I promise."

A woman near the back of the room let out a low satisfied sigh. His smile was welcoming and insulting.

Edith didn't want him to keep talking.

She didn't want to listen to the speech. Now that she knew who he was, Edith pictured herself underneath the table, unbuckling his belt as he pressed against the edge. This could make his presentation a little more enticing. Edith licked her lips as her eyes stared blankly at the table.

Her mental projector played a scene. Her provocative alter ego kneeled. Edith's right hand wrapped around Felix's cock, stroking it slowly. She wanted to run her tongue on his shaft and slobber all over his cock to make him want her again. In her mind, Felix groans and rocks his hips forward and back slightly, teasing her mouth.

Back in reality, Edith inhaled deeply and released a shallow breath. Bianca taps the tip of her pen on the table repeatedly. Are you okay? she mouthed. Edith whispered, "I'm just nervous," Her cheeks warmed up.

"You should be," Felix smirks mischievously. Edith's pussy moistened at the sound of his voice. *I should be sucking your cock right now.* He kept his gaze for a second. "You should be nervous," he looked at the others. "… about the promotion announcements coming at the end of this quarter."

Edith's skin cooled down, and she looked at Felix, confused. Albert and a woman next to him matched her expression.

"Pardon me, sir. Did you say at the end of this quarter?"

Whispers and groans filled the room. Edith was speechless. Felix put his hand down on the table and brushed his pinky against hers. He gave her a quick glance before answering Albert's question.

"That's correct. By the end of December, I should have discussed with your manager about the results."

"That's me," Edith pulled her hand away from his and gestured to herself. "I'm the manager."

"Well, it looks like you'll be in charge, Ms. Rosu," his grin became nauseating to her now. Edith looked at her teammates apologetically. *I'm sorry but I needed this promotion.*

Felix continued to explain what he had hoped to see in the company. He lowered his eyes at everyone and apologized for the inconvenience he might have caused. He mentioned that the Vice President had been absent for three days because of a family emergency and asked him to fill in. Edith locked her eyes at his jawline and watched his lips move. *Did they know about the meeting we had?* She looked up at his eyes then around the room, not wanting to gaze into Felix's eyes anymore.

Felix presented a slideshow, explaining the roles in line for promotion and their benefits. To his luck, they were all excited and taking notes. Edith, however, had her heart lying in the pit of her stomach. A fun, quick fling with the man in front of her turned into a door slammed into her face.

She wanted to move up the ladder and transfer to the next floor of this building, to be with the other directors. Her peers grouped in two and three to discuss the next steps in their upcoming projects.

Felix motioned for her to step out with him into the hallway. With a slight hiss, Edith whispered. "Why didn't you tell me who you were?" she waved her arms around. "Where's the Vice President? Where's Kyle? I need to speak to him now. What if they find out about what we did?" her lips quivered.

Felix put his hands on her shoulders.

"If you calm down, we can work together." he lowered his tone. "No one is going to find out about us. Besides,

I've told you. Kyle had an emergency. He won't be back until Friday."

Edith looked up at him and sighs.

"Bianca's Halloween party is on Friday."

Felix laughs. "Aren't you a little old for parties?" This interaction with the newly identified CEO was light and fun, different from who he was days ago. *He's actually kind of cute*, Edith smiles at him. He looked over at the door and back at Edith. "Are you… needing a date?" he looked down at his shoes.

A date? Edith skipped out on parties and her senior prom. She would be fine without a silly date. Besides, Bianca and the others would have much less to talk about. Edith bit her bottom lip. With her x-ray eyes, she imagined Felix's sculpted body. Going out with someone would be fun for a change. "Um, no. I don't have a date." she paused between each word. Felix's lips shaped. His teeth glistened.

"I'll pick you up on Friday, then. You can give me your phone number after the meeting." he faced his back towards her then turned slightly. "You won't tell on me, right?" Edith had her guard down now. She shook her head. Tell the HR and jeopardize her career? And his? It's too risky. He's the CEO. They'd be happy to laugh in her face.

"You know, I imagined the man who ran this place to be older, sixty maybe?" Edith raised her eyebrows, smirking.

"Ouch," he chuckled.

By the time Felix opened the door, chatter inside the room subsided. Albert and Bianca, barely knowing each other, exchanged looks. Edith sat back down in her seat, just noticing the notepads and pens in front of a few. Since when did they bring those in?

For the rest of the meeting, Felix was the calm and collected boss everyone wanted him to be. He went over the key points of each slide once more and gathered notes that groups wrote. From engineering blueprints of devices to new software programming and accounting, each member of Edith's team was determined to work together while awaiting their promotion results. May the best team builder win. Edith kept her composure around Felix. He's the man, the one they look up to. She's his highly admirable subordinate. Their fling was just part of break time, a onetime thing. Unless, either of them were open to more than just a professional connection.

Edith ran across the street in the rain, clicking her heels. The ice cold water splashed onto her ankles as she became drenched. The forecast this morning said it was cloudy without a chance of rain. She shouldn't have followed that.

She raised both arms above her head and covered it, carefully running in skips. The soles and backs of her feet rubbed against her shoes, but Edith didn't care. She turned right and ran to her car. Edith pulled the keys out from her jacket pocket and pressed a button to unlock. Her car lights lit up, and she headed inside.

The dim sky and thundering rain made her grimace. She pulled the car forward to move away from the work building. Her car ride home was quiet, aside from the violent tapping of rain on the roof and windows. Behind her, a car three feet away honked at another driver. Edith pressed the gas pedal to move a little faster.

At the cross section, a driver on her right was driving carelessly. His speed was slow, but the car swayed back and forth. Edith looked into her rearview and side mirrors. Another driver honked. The impatience of these people; she thought. Without thinking further, Edith turned left. An incoming car headed towards her. Edith's eyes looked straight into the other driver's and she turned the wheel frantically.

Her vision blacked out, and complete silence surrounded her. Voices muffled and yelled outside Edith's car window. Someone stood next to the driver's window with a phone in his hand. A woman near him was in panic, explaining to an operator on her end of the line about what had occurred. Another car parked in front of Edith's with the emergency brake light blinking.

The man knocked on her window.

"Ms. Rosu!" he shouted. Edith's eyes moved around rapidly but her body wouldn't budge. "Ms. Rosu!" he slammed his palm on the window and pulled onto the door handle. "Rosu!"

He continued banging his fist on the window. Edith could hear him, but she was stunned. She imagined herself back at the office with her head laid on the desk. Edith drifted into a deep sleep. The man stared at her body, admiring Edith's face, thinking about how she got herself into this.

He found a rock on the side of the road and picked it up.

At the passenger seat, the mystery man smashed her window and opened the door. Glass shattered, landing on the seat and floor of the car, but barely touched her. Edith muttered something he couldn't understand.

He unbuckled her seatbelt.

"I can't leave you here," he whispered, reaching over to pull her out of the vehicle.

5

Felix put Edith in his bed, staring at her unconscious face. Her skirt hugged her curves but rose as he covered her. *How can she still be unresponsive?* The airbag must have struck pretty hard. This has to be the highlight of Felix's day. Maybe pursuing Edith was a good deed after all.

She muttered in her sleep. Felix chuckled quietly and sat on the floor next to the bed. He rested his chin on his arm, watching the woman breathe peacefully. It wasn't bedtime yet, but something clearly exhausted her from a day's work. "Radley," she groaned. Felix raised his eyebrows. *Are you dreaming about me?*

Edith continued to moan in her sleep.

Felix felt the urge but held himself back. He stood up and left the room, keeping the door open. She'll wake up soon. *I'll give her some space.* He headed back downstairs to the living room and sat in his beloved recliner.

What was I thinking, taking an employee to my house? He sighed and closed his eyes. To be fair, the police or even hospital workers would have asked what he was doing with her had he brought her to the hospital.

He's not the man for her. They both just needed relief from office stress. That's all this is. His mind wandered to his devious undoing. A lonely man like Felix wasn't ready to be in a relationship.

Felix dedicated his life to studies, work, and his business. An arm candy isn't something he'd be interested in right now. One day, I'd be with someone, but not now. She's just a colleague; he thought. He smiles at the ridiculous thought of him being with someone like Edith.

Rumors in the office painted her as the no-nonsense manager. In her eyes, she was in charge and demanded respect. Felix remembered hearing things about her being the best Engineering Manager there is. The office hushed ever since. A track record like hers is what Felix wished to see in others. She was not only beautiful but determined.

Through the years, it seemed like employees turned in their job applications intending to boast to their friends. Felix has been CEO for five years and has had enough of the millennial bragging rights.

Felix walked to the kitchen and tipped the pitcher to pour himself a glass of ice-cold water. Now wasn't the time to reminisce about being a young hard-working man. *There's a woman upstairs in your bedroom.* He chugged the water and stepped casually up the stairs, taking his time to greet his unexpected guest.

Fully quenched and awake, Felix entered the room in time to see Edith facing the door with her hands tucked under her cheek. She looked like an angel, gracefully sleeping in the bed of a king.

He caught himself studying her, listening to her breath. She groaned again in her sleep. Something about this caused his heart to pound and bang at his rib cage.

Felix cleared his throat and set the glass down on the dresser.

6

Edith blinked. She looked to her left, squinting. This isn't my house. Her eyes moved around, eyeing the coffee table next to her and the dining table at a distance. Someone kidnapped me. She flinched and hissed, putting a hand on her forehead. Edith closed her eyes and laid still.

She clutched onto the comforter and pressed her hand on the silk blue sheets, that rubbed against her skin.

"Morning, sleepyhead," A figure stepped into the light. Edith squinted her eyes, realizing that the light wasn't as bright as she thought it was. She squinted and blinked some more.

"Albert?"

She was stunned and her head spun a little.

"It's me," The man sat, resting her legs on his lap.

"Felix?" Her pupils dilated as she looked around, feeling her heart race. "Mr. Radley! What am I doing here? What happened?"

"Shh. You're alright. You crashed your car a block away from work." he said, adjusting his posture. "You're lucky I found you when I was walking to my car. The ambulance was on their way, but I told the officers that I knew you."

"What? Why? What did you say?"

"I told them you were my girlfriend." he rolled his eyes. "They bought it and so I took you here. To my place."

He pulled the curtains open revealing trees and letting moonlight in. Edith expected the room to have clothes lazily tossed in the laundry hamper or a pair of boxers on the floor. Everything was neatly organized. *He must have hired a housekeeper.*

Felix Radley continuously amused her. In a second, he was daring and dominant, taking her body into his and claiming her. Then, a week later, he became the loving Clark Kent type of guy. Edith saw the way the intern stared at him earlier. He was being Mr. Perfect. Edith directed her thoughts to the workload she was supposed to complete by this weekend.

Edith transported herself elsewhere. Felix stood up and pulled off his long sleeve shirt. His scent raised the hairs on her arms. Her eyes looked at his lips and down at his crotch. He hovered on top of her and brought his face closer to hers. "Your car will be at the shop for a while, so you're stuck with me." Felix's warm breath smelled like peppermint. He cleared his throat. "Edith," he says.

"Yes?"

"Now that you know I'm the CEO, no one can know about us being together, okay?"

"Together?" she flushed. *Why would I want to tell anyone? Who would I tell?*

"I never had a woman stay at my house before, but you're an exception,"

Edith watched his lips and lunged, swinging her arms around his neck. She could feel him smiling as she pressed a wet, longing kiss onto his lips. The sliding door blinds were wide open and neither of them cared. Felix moaned lightly as he sank into her lips deeper.

Edith eagerly dipped her tongue into his mouth, tasting him. He also closed his eyes, taking it in.

The softness of his lips brought her thoughts to the office floor. Before all this, Edith didn't know she had an office kink, that she and the CEO would be frolicking. It didn't take long for him to show her what she needed. Between gasps and moans, Edith's legs spread wider, inviting Felix in between her legs. Her skirt rose and the fabric of his jeans reddened her thighs.

His hand ran up the side of her thigh and went further up to touch her ass. "Mmm," she moaned. His left hand gave her cheek a small squeeze. Just then, a vibration coming from the top of the dining table interrupted them.

"It's your phone," he breathed.

Felix gently moved aside for Edith to get up and take the call. She walked over to the table and picked up the phone. It was the insurance company detailing information about the towing and the caller informed it would take at least two weeks for a repair. The call was brief and Edith scrolled through her phone for emails and voicemail messages.

The officer on her case left an emailed summary and contact information. *I should handle this later*. She locked and placed her phone down on the table and noticed her purse strap hung on the chair. It was almost like she was at home. Felix walked up behind her and kissed the right of her neck slowly. Edith's neck tickled, and she turned around to put her right hand on his face. Felix planted a soft kiss on her lips, pecking two, three times.

She wanted him to devour her.

Felix slips his hands under her and wraps Edith in his arms. She's swept off the couch as he carried her up the stairs. Edith placed her hands on his shoulders, keeping her balance. Felix's forearms tensed, ensuring she was safe.

There was a door on the left and another on the right. A door in front of the staircase led to the bathroom. Felix carried Edith to the left. "The other room is my office," he says. With a free hand, he twisted the doorknob and lazily kicked the door open. It was a large master bedroom with emerald green walls and sandpaper-colored floors.

There were white double-doors for the walk-in closet and a single door for his bathroom. Felix must have liked the color gray. There was a wooden dresser with photos of him as a child and teenager. Felix placed something on the dresser and looked at Edith. Her eyes noted everything.

Against the wall was his bed with a wooden gray headboard. Silk navy blue sheets wrapped around the mattress and matched the pillows. Expensive tastes; she thought. Felix laid Edith on the right side of the bed, turned the lamp on, and pulled the gray duvet above her.

He walked over to the window and pulled the curtains closed.

"You can sleep here tonight," he says, turning and crawling on top of the bed. He laid down and leaned on his elbow, staring at Edith.

"Where are you going to sleep? This is your house. I couldn't possibly sleep here."

"I know there isn't much space but I can sleep on the couch tonight."

"How can I change clothes? There's nothing else to wear."

He narrowed his eyes and patted her arm.

"I saw your body. You can sleep naked."

Edith smirked back, mirroring his smile. Felix, technically being her boss, gave her an order. Were they going to talk about their first encounter? The heat between them was being neutralized by the cold sheets. Edith turned on her side and ran her finger over the fabric.

"I want you to lie with me and stay awhile. What did I do to get you so aroused?" she batted her eyes. Felix pressed his lips, trying not to smile.

"What do you mean?" he raised his eyebrows.

"You know, that day when I was supposed to be at a meeting,"

He played it cool, going into his thoughts. I knew you were coming, Edith. I needed to have you. My cock demanded it. She smiles slyly. "You had a meeting?" he paused. Edith inhaled slowly, thinking about him touching her. "Maybe I faked that meeting to lure you in."

Edith's eyes widened.

"You mean I woke up early for nothing?" she gasped.

Felix kissed her softly, keeping the smile on his face. "It wasn't for nothing. You woke up early because I needed my breakfast." he planted another kiss on her lips and moved away.

"I have never seen you around before. No one mentions you, not even the other managers." Felix laid flat on his back and fluffed his pillow.

"I'm a private guy. I'll pop in and make rounds but I must avoid announcing myself because people can pry. No one dares talk about me unless they want to sleep on the streets."

Edith gulped at his comment and let out a satisfied sigh. "I think you just made work more interesting for me."

If there was an actual meeting, she might not have met Felix nor had seen the excitement and appreciation in the eyes of her peers. This was fate.

The following day, Felix dropped Edith at her house. They enter the house and Felix looked around. It was a lot smaller and more cozy than his. The house had light oak wood flooring and creme-colored walls for the living room. The kitchen was lime-green, perfect for the sunlight to enter.

Edith blushes and looks across the room at her bedroom door. "Just stay here and make yourself feel at home. I'll be right back." she says.

Edith wasn't fond of contemporary aesthetic. A white vintage fabric couch centered in the living room with an old coffee table and a TV stand. The only thing modern in here was the LED TV. There was a short tattered bookshelf next to the stand, filled with classic novels. A smile curved on Felix's lips when he saw Shakespeare's Romeo and Juliet.

Her house was a town over from their work building. It must have taken an hour or two for Edith to commute each day. Felix lived fifteen minutes away. Edith gazed at her bed, wishing she and Felix were lying down talking or putting their hands on each other like horny teenagers. She went to her closet and pulled clothes for the office, then moved to the drawers for undergarments and sleepwear.

Felix was on the couch reading one of her books when she stepped out with a medium purple suitcase.

"Ready for your flight to my house?" he says with the right corner of his mouth curving upward. Edith looked at her suitcase and back at Felix.

"Wait a second, Superman." she laughed. "Since I'm here, you can just go," she said with a straight face, placing her hands on her hips.

He moves to take the suitcase from her. "But your house is two hours away from the office. We work different hours, Edith. It'll be fine. We're going."

Edith dropped her shoulders and took her keys from the coffee table.

She couldn't argue with him about that. It would be a pain for him to drive over and act as her chauffeur, and a two-hour bus ride would be time-consuming. Felix takes her hand and pulls her outside before she changed her mind again.

They entered his car, and the ride was quiet on the way back. Along the way, traffic had slowed them down. Two police cars arrived to investigate a road rage incident four blocks away from Felix's home. Edith stared out the window and something came to mind.

"Felix, what are we?"

"What?" he asked, gripping onto the steering wheel. His eyes flashed over to Edith.

"What are we? We're just coworkers, right?"

Felix kept his eyes on the road, but his heart pumped. *I'm just being a nice man, right?* As much as he enjoyed the kissing and touching, he never thought about being in a relationship. Was he ready for commitment? Was she?

"We are coworkers, yes." he answered, filling in the silence. Coworkers professionally and to everyone else, but after hours, there had to be something else between them. "Edith, if you're not comfortable with me—"

"I won't report you, Felix. It's just that I knew you for a day," she paused. "Three days now… and things are moving so fast between us." her lips grew dry as she spoke.

"Edith, if I didn't like you, I wouldn't have saved you," he said. Her eyes dropped to her lap.

The traffic ahead of them moved. A traffic officer stepped out to the side to guide moving cars. He smiles at Edith through the window. She barely noticed while speaking to Felix. He could have liked her. The rush didn't give her much time to think about her own feelings for him. In her mind, what they did was a one and done incident.

7

The silk sheets ruffled underneath Edith's back. Sleeping on her side, Edith bit her lip to keep the drool from spilling out of her mouth. Her eyelids stayed shut as her eyes moved around impatiently.

She wanted Felix to lie in bed next to her, but he kept his word, sleeping on the sofa downstairs. To her surprise, it was a sleeper sofa pulled out to convert into a bed. Had he planned this? Edith was deep into her dream state.

Images of Felix typing away on his keyboard at his office played. The office walls were a cloudy white, but everything else was in color. Edith looked at the man sitting at his desk. Is that Felix? she thought. She crept closer to clear her vision. Part of her brain was sure that Felix was sound asleep in the house. Her subconsciousness wanted her to experience him in a dream too.

He barely blinked, curving his eyebrows at the words appearing on the screen. His deep sigh prompted Edith to step into the room.

"Did you want to see me, Sir?" she pressed her lips, shyly avoiding his gaze. Why am I calling him "Sir"? she thought.

This was her first time being here. The walls were light gray with white trims. He had an espresso-colored dresser and an Apple computer sat on his desk with a navy blue mat. *What is happening?* Edith wanted to wake up.

"Edith, thank you for coming. Please. Come in and shut the door." he lifted his head, looking above the monitor. Watching as she followed his order. "I wanted to congratulate you for your promotion. Kyle, Eric, and I are thrilled to have you on the floor."

Edith sat on the chair in front of his desk.

"Thank you, Mr. Radley."

He smiles and exhales through his nose then steps around to sit on the corner of his desk. His knee barely touched hers. Felix glanced at the door and windows. Edith watched as he walked over and pulled the blinds down, dimming the sunlight.

"When you're here in my office, Edith, I want you to call me Felix." he says, turning. She could only see the side of his face. A hint of darkness presented in his eye.

"Of course, sir." she hesitated and bit her dry lip. "Felix,"

She would never call authority by their first name. He was her boss and everyone should give him respect. Why should he be casual with her? Felix fully turned and approached her chair. She looked up, trying to calm her nerves.

"Is there anything else?"

"You're beautiful, Edith. I hope you know that," he says.

Felix lightly pressed his thumb on her chin, using his hand to lift it. He leans down. Edith's heart wanted to leap out of her chest.

"Felix," she whispered.

He fully put his lips on hers, kissing her softly. She inhales nervously, then moans into his mouth as he kissed her again.

Edith gasped and sat up straight. She blinked as light from the hall entered the room. Felix walks in and kneels next to the bed, watching Edith's chest rise and fall. Her eyes dilated upon seeing him and she blinked at him, confused.

"Hi, Felix," she says groggily, lying on her back, creating an indent. "What are you doing here?" She squints, shielding the light from her eyes, and pulls the blanket up to her chest. Felix smiles and breathes calmly. "I wanted to check on you," he tucks hair behind her ears. "I went to the bathroom and heard you mumbling my name." Felix chuckles and rests his arms on the edge of the bed.

Should she lie? Sweat dripped down her chest from the thick blanket covering her body. She pulled it down and looked into his eyes. "I was... dreaming about you," she groaned slightly.

Her cheeks flushed red, and the blanket didn't do a good job of covering her embarrassment. He stares into her eyes, curious about this dream of hers. His eyebrows perked up, but his cock hardened as well, knowing where this was going.

He stretched his arm, putting his hand on her hip.

"Tell me about this dream of yours."

"It's silly. It's nothing important, really."

Felix's eyes dilated. "I'm sure it wasn't terrible. You can tell me about it. I'm all ears." he licked his lips, pressing onto his arm as he moved closer to the bed.

"I was in your office,"

"On the sixth floor?" he asks, curving his eyebrows. "What could you be doing there?"

A grin crept on his face, and he caressed her hip. I know what you're trying to do; Edith thought. It was working.

"You wanted to talk with me. In my dream, they promoted me as director and you wanted to congratulate me." she said, trying to steady her breath.

He moved his hand up her hip and teasingly touched the side of her pelvis. Edith's face heated more. Can she just end her story and have him leave the room? His touch was increasing her arousal. She glanced down to see his erection.

"Is that all?"

"You told me to call you by your first name, and then you kissed me." Edith pressed her lips. She sighed in relief from getting the words out.

"Hmm, that sounds like a boring dream." he moved to stand up.

Edith blinked to see Felix tucking his thumbs into the side of his pajama bottoms. Edith's eyes widened at the sight. Her heart pounded and her pussy twitched in excitement, a feeling that she didn't think she would have upon waking up.

"What are you doing?" Felix's lips curved upward.

"I don't think your dream had a proper ending."

"Felix," she groaned.

He pulled his pants and boxers down, allowing them to touch the rug. Edith pressed her lips, unsure of what to do.

"Felix," she repeated.

"This is my house and my rules, Edith. If I'm going to be your boss, you'll have to listen to me."

Edith wished she had mentioned nothing. Her dream was a fantasy. They may have fucked once, but she didn't think there would be a continuation. If he was going to be her boss, she would need to be precautious about something like this, right? She looked at him without another thought coming to mind.

Edith pulled the blanket off, revealing her bare skin. She got down on her knees on the rug in front of her boss. He might as well be her master.

"Good girl, I would like for you to maintain following orders." he looked down at her.

This third version of Felix, that Edith noted, was raising the bar. He was the devil in a suit. With such power and control, he could command her to do anything, and all she could do was obey.

"Now, minx, I want you to take my cock in your mouth and suck."

Her top teeth slide on her bottom lip, wanting to say Felix, but there was no use in objecting his wishes. One, two, three, Edith counted. She wrapped her lips around his cock, with her lips rubbing against his shaft. Her mouth drooled as she thought about him kissing her needy lips. Felix breathes softly. He breathed harder when Edith held his cock in her hand and glide her tongue up and around the head.

Felix pushed her head, forcing his cock back inside her mouth and her hand drops. She groans as the taste of his skin met with her tongue.

"Now Edith, place your hands on your lap." he commanded.

He moved his hips forward and back to begin. She puts her palms on her knees and sucks on his cock harder. He gently grabs the back of her hair and moves his hips back and forth faster. Her slurps and gags caused the beast inside him to force her to do more. Felix clutched onto Edith's auburn hair, making her groan. He moved faster, sliding his cock in and out of her mouth. Suck me, you slut. His balls hit her chin, but she couldn't object.

Willingly, Edith wiggled and flicked her tongue as he worked her mouth. Her pussy folds moistened, wishing to be plowed by this godly boss to be. She was definitely the leading candidate for the position. She might have been the only candidate, and everyone else was a decoy. The thought of her winning increased her pleasure. It increased her desire to please Felix.

"I'm almost there. Keep going," he says. He used both hands to grab onto her locks, pushing and pulling at her hair to increase the motion. The wetness of her mouth and tongue rubbing against the veins of his cock called for ejaculation. "Fuck Edith, it's coming." he thrusted into her mouth, moaning quietly. Spurts of his cum spilled onto her tongue and she swallowed while gagging. Edith groaned, allowing his cum to run down her throat.

Felix knelt in front of Edith. The lust in his eyes spread fire on her skin. She looked up at him, pressing her lips and waiting for the next command. He leans down and lifts her chin with his hand.

"Are you ready for the next thing, slut?"

Edith pouted, wanting more. She nods. He looked down at his crotch as it twitches with excitement. Felix takes her hand to assist her back up.

"Bend over the edge of the bed." he says with a light whisper. His tone was harsh yet soft.

Edith bends over the edge with her knees shaking. She exhaled and stretched her arms on the bed, lightly clutching on the blue silk. It wrinkles in her hands. Felix leans down to her ear and kisses her left cheek. His scent overpowers her.

"Felix," she breathes.

"I'm going to fuck you so hard,"

His words sent ripples of adrenaline through her pussy. She pictured being pinned down over the espresso desk in her dream. Felix positions himself and rubs his index finger on her slit. It moistens and cum drips onto his fingers. He slides and sticks the finger in her, making the cum pop like gum. Felix teases with another finger in then yanks both fingers out, putting them to his lips. Edith listens as he licks her juice. He moans, "You're a bad girl, Ms. Rosu."

He rubs the tip of his cock on her slit again. The hole opens and welcomes the cock's head. Edith kept her eyes closed, feeling Felix's cock enter slowly. During the first time, it was spontaneous and head-spinning. He shoved his cock inside and rammed incredibly fast. Her pussy enjoyed that feeling. The texture of his cock and the pulsing of his veins were things to remember.

This time, Felix was careful and purposely teasing her body. He wanted her to beg. Beg for me, she heard him say in her mind. Edith perks her ass a little and pushes against him gently. Felix blinked in surprise and grinned.

"If you want more, tell me." he breathed into her ear.

He ached to thrust immediately, but it's all part of the game. I'll make her want me; he thought. Edith whined.

"Mr. Radley, please." she moans.

Calling him Mr. Radley hinted of submission. She is the subordinate, after all. He inches inside slowly and pulls out to make her lose it. She lifted her head and looked at him.

"Please what, Ms. Rosu?" he leaned, brushing his nose behind her ear. "

Please. Fuck me, Mr. Radley. I need you. I need your cock." her tone was close to a whimper.

Felix places a pillow in front of her to rest her chest on. He inhaled slowly and shoved his cock inside her. Edith's body didn't hesitate to shiver and cum in an instant. He was torturing her, and it was worth every second. He moved in and out carefully to take in the pleasure. Edith thought he was actually backing out. She lifted her head and turned to look at him. The devilish grin on his face confirmed it was only beginning. Felix looked deeply into her eyes and gave his hardest thrust.

"Oh, Felix!" she moaned, shutting her eyes.

"What happened to Mr. Radley?"

His joke was sensual and arousing. Edith bit her lip down to stop the smile from curving. He moved faster and harder, desiring her screams. Felix took a step further and grabbed her hair into his fist.

"Ah!" she gasped. "I'll be gentle,"

He made quick motions, hitting her walls. Edith internally screamed as pleasure surged through her. The moans became louder, and she wanted to tone it down. He's so good at this. Felix loved the sound of her moans and screams, permitting him to increase his stamina. The beast inside him has woken up from its slumber. Each thrust sent Edith spiraling. Her hips and pelvis ached. He was eagerly trying to squeeze every drop of cum out of her. "You're my minx now, Ms. Rosu; filthy slut." he growls slightly.

He smacked her ass hard, releasing a squeal out of Edith's mouth. She moved back and forth, meeting with each thrust and Felix continues to smack her ass, thinking it would produce more excitement out of her. She squealed and moaned, not wanting a drop of spit on the precious silk sheets.

Felix grabs onto Edith's arms, pinning on the bed as it shook. By now, her knees were hitting against the side of the mattress and turning red. Edith could only feel the thrill that she desperately needed. The more thrusts he made, the more she wanted. She wanted to feel every inch of this man's hardness. Four more, five more thrusts caused Edith to lose all her senses. He brazenly tossed her innocence and professionalism out the window.

"I'm all yours, Mr. Radley! Fuck Felix, take me!"

With that, he pumped and gave her his all. Felix reached over and covered her mouth with his right hand, still thrusting as she squirted, splashing on his cock and down her thighs. He moved swiftly, unloading his own cum into her. Edith groans into his hand. Her muffles became inaudible.

"How's that for being the man of your dreams?" he asks.

Felix pulled out and lifted Edith onto the bed. His own words made him flush pink.

Edith moved to sleep on her side. She licked her lips and closed her eyes. Felix kissed her on the forehead and put his arm around her before falling asleep.

8

Edith pouted, looking through the clothes rack Felix bought for her. He hadn't thought about where she'd be putting her things, so the collapsable rack in his bedroom was a temporary solution. This is insane; she thought. Felix entered the room holding a small box and a gray tie on top of it. He glanced at the bed as it had a shirt and pants laid out on top.

Felix could hear the scraping of the metal hooks.

"Is everything okay?" Felix asked.

He placed his newly purchased items on top of the dresser and stood behind Edith inside the closet. She was on the floor, groaning and sighing, she rolled her eyes up to the ceiling and flickered them at him. Felix raised his eyebrows.

"Bianca's party is tomorrow, and I have nothing to wear. The event slipped my mind."

"You don't have to wear anything," he grinned, holding back a laugh. Edith shot a look at him and his eyes directed at a blue fit and flare dress. "What do you normally wear to work?"

"Either a blouse and skirt or a dress, but that's rare. I wear pants occasionally."

Felix chuckled at her comment and pulled the blue dress from the clothes rack. The skirt was just above the knee. Edith watched him stare at the dress, knowing his favorite color was blue.

"Wear this," he says.

Edith stands up to meet him.

"It's too formal for a party."

"It's still appropriate for a work party. I want to show you something."

Felix takes the dress in his arm and holds Edith's hand. He leads her to the box on the dresser and picks up the tie.

"You want to show me your tie?"

Felix smirked. "Open the box."

She looks at him, then takes the box. Edith gently took the cover off to reveal two filigree metal masquerade masks. Felix picked out a black mask with gold accents for himself and Edith's mask was plain gold.

"I couldn't figure out what to wear either, but I got these for us," he said.

Felix slowly put his mask on like a madman, but he was too sexy and charming to be evil. Edith stood in front of the body mirror and held the dress in front of her, picturing how she would look as if she were going to a billionaire's ball. Felix stood behind her and kissed her on the cheek. He raised the mask in front of her eyes. Edith admired the gold tone reflecting and matching her eyes. Felix then lowered the mask.

He pressed into her with his crotch against her ass, and whispered in her ear. "Wear this dress so I can recognize you at the party," His voice sent electricity down her spine, and the minty feel from his breath cooled her earlobe.

"Okay," she nodded. "I will,"

Edith moved to hang the dress on the closet door hook. Felix licked his lips, wanting to strip Edith despite her putting on clothes minutes before.

She cleared her throat and turned around in time to have Felix pin her back against the wall. She breathed out his name and his hands on her sides, reaching down her hips.

Felix kissed Edith from the neck up, planting his warm touch on her clavicle and trailing up her neck. Edith gasped and groaned. She wiggled her hips to shake the building arousal between her legs. Felix smiles and licked Edith's lips while kissing her passionately.

There were three things he planned to do at that Halloween party. One, to blend in with his peers and see what they're like. Middle to elderly aged men have only surrounded him. Edith opened his eyes to knowing what millennials like himself were doing. Two, Felix wanted to make sure Edith was enjoying herself. When he observed her colleagues during that meeting, Bianca had surely ticked him off. Albert was one of the loyal employees and a good guy. What if Bianca was a bad influence? His third reason tied to the second. Felix wanted a part two of their office devilment.

Edith strutted toward the sidewalk wearing the blue dress and mask. She paired the ensemble with a petite black blazer and black velvet ankle strap heels. Her hair was wavy and clipped on the back. She felt as if she were attending a gala and not at an office party.

Felix and Edith agreed to drive solo so no one at the office could see them together. He walked eight feet behind her, listening to her heels click on the cement and watching her hips sway as she walked. He looked back and to his right to see if anyone from the building was around.

Cameras never lie, although he doubted that security guards would watch footage and make a comment.

Edith opened the doors, and the dark lobby made her feel unsettled. She was used to the chatter, listening to men in suits talk about their investments. Edith rubbed her shoulder as she pressed the elevator button.

Felix entered the building nonchalantly and pretended not to know her. Edith looked behind her, staring at the lounge armchair that Felix sat in weeks before, gazing at her body. He cleared his throat and stepped behind her, tilting his head to look at the door light. The doors opened, and he gestured for her to go in first. A sense of déjà vu smacked Edith in the gut.

The two entered the elevator, and Edith pressed the button for the fifth floor. Felix made a slight chuckle, and Edith glanced over at him. Instead of saying a word, he pulled out his phone and texted her phone.

The phone vibrates in her jacket pocket, and she looked at the screen.

I'm tempted to touch you again... here and now.

Edith sucked in her teeth and Felix didn't mind releasing his inner demon at work. She glanced at him and he returned a malicious gaze.

Edith typed quickly.

Something tells me you made plans for tonight.

He looked up at her and smiles, typing back.

You're not wrong.

The ride on the elevator was slow and silent, but a few more long breaths and they had made it to the fifth floor. Felix allowed Edith to walk ahead of him again. She walked down the hallway confidently, and he stood by the elevator doors. Edith's group set up the decor and food placements past the conference rooms, so it was quite the walk.

Lights flickered above her as she took a step. Edith wondered if this was part of the Halloween spirit.

Past the cubicle, she could see someone wearing a witch hat standing next to the Pillsbury Doughboy. She laughed lightly because she rarely saw men on this floor stand up. They were always sitting at their cubicles when she arrived at work.

The rough carpet made it difficult to walk faster, so she took larger steps. Bianca walked out from the crowd and turned to see Edith trying her best to get to them all.

"Edith! You're here!" she yelled, throwing her arms for a hug. "What are you wearing?" she gazed at Edith's outfit.

"I'm a masquerade ball attendee,"

Bianca chuckled. She wore a slim silver dress and leggings. A pair of sky blue wings were riding on her back. She waved at Albert and pulled Edith toward the crowd.

"Look who's here!" Bianca said, grinning.

"Ms. Rosu, you made it!"

Albert was holding a red cup in one hand and his arm was around a woman who Edith couldn't recognize. She had medium tone skin and straight blonde hair that reached down to her hips. All she wore was a neon green dress and brown ankle boots.

"Please Albert, you can call me Edith for today." He tilted his cup at her and smiles.

"This is my girlfriend, Candy. She's my Tinker Bell." he said proudly.

It took a second for Edith to gather her thoughts.

Bianca tapped on Edith's shoulder and had her turn. Edith half-smiles and Bianca looked her up and down.

"I like your outfit." she said. Edith unbuttoned her blazer to reveal her dress. "What are you supposed to be? A secret investor? Your mask looks expensive."

Felix walks in casually. No one seemed to notice him except for Edith and Bianca. "Excuse me, ladies." he says, walking to the snack table.

The music playing was so loud that Bianca couldn't recognize his voice. He walked over to the punch bowl and poured himself a drink, then grabbed some chips and salsa. Felix glanced over at Edith, making her cheeks turn pink. The lights were dim enough to hide her expression.

"Who is that guy?" Bianca leaned over to ask.

"I don't know," Edith forced her lips into a straight line.

"That's so funny. You're both wearing masks."

Edith watched as the CEO of the company walked around, mingling and complimenting each person's costume. Was there a contest Edith was unaware of? She furrowed her eyebrows and licked her lips as her stomach growled. Edith grabbed herself a plate of mini prawn cocktail papadum.

Georgia, one coder on the floor, smiles at Edith's choice of food. She must have been the one who brought them.

The other engineers, Britney and Evan walked around with trays of more finger food. Edith groaned, wanting more than just two bites. She looked at Felix, who was enjoying himself; walking around as the entire meal. Women giggled and listened intently as he spoke to them.

Edith shoved her jealously down by pouring herself a cup of soda and chugging it.

Albert nodded his head at Edith, lifting a bottle of apple cider. Edith mindlessly walked over to him and he poured her a drink into a plastic wine glass.

"Who's your friend, Edith?"

"What?" she choked.

One drop of cider glided down her throat. She stared at Albert in horror. Albert's girlfriend walked away to converse with other people. Edith took her place and stood next to him.

"You keep looking at that guy over there. Do you know him?"

They both stared at Felix. Edith was feeling hot enough to strip her blazer off. She held the jacket in her arm.

"I don't know him at all." She raised an eyebrow.

Albert smiles. "If you say so,"

Edith chugged the apple cider and excused herself, licking her lips and wiping the spill off her chin.

Albert and Bianca watched as she stepped out of the space and walked down the hallway. She turned to her left for the women's restroom. Her subconscious was betraying her. No one was supposed to know about her and Felix. They were smarter than she thought, regardless of their words being assumptions.

She hung her jacket on the wall hook, looked into the mirror, and turned the faucet on. Running the water on her wrists, Edith thought about her promotion again. What would they say if someone found out about her connection with the CEO? Somebody would love to take down Felix for good. She exhaled deeply and turned the sink off. Edith grabbed her jacket and walked out.

Felix had his back leaning against the wall. He was looking down at his shoes. He looked at Edith with curved eyebrows.

"I saw you walk out of there. Are you okay? Did something happen?"

He stepped forward, took the jacket from her, and put a hand on her arm. Edith looked up at him.

"I don't think this thing between us is going to work."

"How do you mean?"

"I don't want any trouble. Someone could report you. They'd report both of us."

"Edith, I won't let that happen. But if it comes to that, I wouldn't mind leaving the company."

"You wouldn't?"

"No, and I'll be taking you with me." he said. The corner of Edith's mouth twitched into a smirk. He placed his hand on her cheek. "Your face is so warm. I think we both need to get out of here. Let's go upstairs to my office."

She looked at him and bit down on her tongue to avoid saying something. Felix and Edith walked discreetly to the staircase, not wanting to risk being seen in the elevator together. Walking four floors up wasn't a problem for Felix; his legs could power through. As they stepped up, Felix looked at Edith. *I could give her a piggyback*. He shook his head.

"You know," he said. Felix's voice echoed. "You haven't properly introduced yourself to me." Edith's eyes widened. She didn't think he'd care about her personal life. "You know a bit about my family. What about yours?"

Edith stopped her tracks and held onto the railing. Being a step higher, Felix looked down at her.

"There's not a lot to know about me." she said, continuing her step. "My parents moved from Romania to Boston. They had me, then I worked at fourteen to help make ends meet." she blinked at Felix, who listened intently, wanting to hear more.

"Did you study here in Boston?" he asked, swallowing dryly.

Edith nodded. "I graduated from high school a year earlier than everyone else and attended college at seventeen. Then, I applied for a program to get my Master's early as well."

Felix's heart pounded, knowing that he fucked an ambitious and mesmerizing woman. Sure, he's inherited money and now owns the company, but school was a nightmare for Felix. Why desire someone like him if she was so intelligent? He pressed his lips to stop the frown.

"I heard great things about a woman who worked here. It just didn't occur to me that the woman was you," Felix flashes a smile. "I wish I had met you sooner, Edith." he reached out his hand for her to take and helped her up to walk with him.

If that were the case, we would have fucked sooner, Mr. Radley. Edith's cheeks turned red. "That's the first time you said my first name in a while." *I like that.*

"I'll say it more, then," his response made her face grow warmer.

As the two walked up the stairs, Felix talked about his little sister being care free and wanting to go with him to the park each weekend.

When they were young, their parents would take them by the lake or attend carnivals as a family. Lola was nine at the time of her death, and Felix was twelve. His heart sank as he told Edith about her.

Edith didn't know what it was like to have a sibling. Her parents had only planned to have one child, and she wanted to make them proud by going up the career ladder. Edith told Felix that her parents had moved back to Romania for their retirement years ago.

Before moving back to Massachusetts, Felix didn't know what to do with his life. When there were no jobs available after college, Felix's uncle became his crutch, sharing wealth until receiving an inheritance from his grandmother's passing.

Felix's eyes watered. He kept his gaze straight ahead so Edith wouldn't see his pain. Edith was a self-made woman, working from the ground up, something that Felix hadn't heard of from any woman he's met. He cleared his throat and held onto Edith's hand, pulling her up the stairs with him. Edith's phone buzzed inside her pocket, and she checks it. Bianca messaged her.

Where are you?

Felix lowered Edith's hand.

"Don't answer that," he says.

In no time, they made it to the sixth floor. Felix joked about carrying Edith down the hallway because of her slow pace. As all floors, the sixth floor was pitch black and cold from the air-conditioning.

In her years of working at Brighton, she had only passed through the sixth floor to assist the managers. She never interacted with the directors and the CEO rarely crossed her mind. She gazed at the driftwood gray walls and plants that sat on top of the shelf. Leaves wilted down to the wooden floor.

Felix closed the door behind him and pulled the blinds down, just like he did in Edith's dream. She pulled the mask off her face, revealing her gold eyeshadow blended with brown. Felix stepped in front of her, looking into her eyes.

He pulled off his own mask and exhaled.

"Well, we're here in my office. Like what you see?" he said, grinning.

"The walls were gray in my dream," she chuckles.

Edith imagined his assistants walking into this office and blushing, wanting to try something with Felix. Edith wanted to walk into this office freely one day, but she wasn't at his level.

For a tech CEO, Felix's office was quite regal, with a vintage end table and bookshelf. For a contemporary touch, Felix added a coffee machine. He must have spent time long enough in his office to think of having a coffee machine. The desk and office chair were like what Edith saw in her dream. He caught her gaze and stood in front of her, putting his hands on her hips.

"You have an amazing office, Felix."

"I'm thrilled to have you here. Now that we're here, is there anything you want to talk about? Anything you want to do, perhaps?"

Felix studied Edith before pulling her close, keeping her in his grasp.

9

Edith woke up on the Monday after her forgotten weekend with the blanket below her waist. Days were rolling by and another work-loaded week awaited her. While her peers honored the weekends, Edith wanted to work.

She stepped out of bed, wrapping a throw blanket she picked up from Felix's closet around her bare skin. She clutched onto the fabric while carefully walking down the stairs. Felix was at the table, staring at his laptop screen.

"Good-morning," he says, peeking above the laptop.

"Morning, Felix," she paused and looked over at a plate of pancakes on the kitchen counter. "What time is it?"

"9:47 A.M." a smile spread across his face.

"I'm late! Why didn't you wake me?"

Edith's eyes were ready to bulge out.

"You don't have to worry. Have some breakfast with me. I had my assistant tell your manager you'll be working from home today."

Her cheeks turned back to their normal color. She curved her eyebrows.

"That makes little sense. Wouldn't they wonder how your assistant knew me? I didn't even know you had an assistant." she formed her lips into a pout.

Felix scooted his chair back and guided Edith to sit on his lap. He buried his face into her tangled hair.

"You'll be working from home today. Victoria can just say that you two network together. You'll meet her eventually." he says, embracing Edith's waist. He chuckles, and she gets off his lap. "Wait here," he gestured.

Felix jogged up the stairs and entered his bedroom. He returned holding a gray plush robe in his arm. Edith drops the blanket on the floor and Felix nibbles his bottom lip.

"Wear this robe for now. You need to eat." He holds the robe out for Edith to slip her arms through the holes. She wrapped it around and tied the belt while serving herself a plate of food.

"One day, I'll have to cook for you." she says, glancing at him. "I'd like to see what you have in mind," he replied. Felix watched as Edith took a bite of her over easy eggs. She continued to split a piece of bacon in half and cut her pancake. "If you want to use my office upstairs, you can. I'm sure they sent you something to do today."

"That'd be lovely. Thank you,"

Edith took her time eating breakfast. She rarely worked from home, but she couldn't object. Her team was alert, ambitious, and always hustling. Albert and Bianca were typically the only two with questions to ask.

Edith was simply their friend and facilitator.

She scraped the last piece of egg yolk off the plate with a spoon and licked it off with one swipe in her mouth. Felix watched as the yolk dripped onto her chin. He took a napkin from the kitchen counter and wiped the yolk off her skin.

"My breakfast is that good, huh?" he chuckled. "Let's go upstairs now to set up for your work."

Edith nodded and pushed the chair back to get up from the table. Felix gestures for her to walk in front of him. The round shape of her ass was in full view. Being the animal that he was, Felix swallowed and cleared his throat as he pictured Edith naked and kneeling.

She turned to her left and walked up the steps. Felix kept his eyes on the top of the stairs as he followed her to the office.

"To your right," he said.

She turned and opened the frosted glass panel door. The room was larger than Edith's guest bathroom. Felix's office nearly resembled her work office, with the desk centered in the middle. However, the bookshelf was on the left of the entrance. There's a plant in the corner where Edith's bean bag chair would be. Behind the desk was a wide console table.

On top were four photo frames. There was one photo of an old couple, a golden retriever, a young girl, and the last frame on the right was of Felix in his high school years. Felix walked over to his computer in a hurry. Edith crossed her arms to soothe herself as she waited.

She looked down at her feet, tapping her toes on the soft cream-colored carpet. She looked up and fixated on the photos again.

"Is that your family?" she asked.

"What?"

"Behind you, the people in the photos. Are they relatives of yours?"

Edith blushed.

She didn't want to get into his personal life too soon, but the photos piqued her curiosity. Felix tapped at his keyboard loudly. His eyes shifted from the computer screen to the photos, and up at Edith, meeting her eyes.

"Um, yeah," he said, pressing a key twice and clicking on the mouse. "Those are my parents and sister."

The corner of Edith's mouth moved upward.

"I see," she crossed her arms and rubbed her elbows to self-soothe. "Are they here in Boston?" she swallowed.

"Okay," he said, evading the question. "You can log into Slack now." Felix said roughly. He smiles lightly, pulling the office chair out for Edith to sit.

"You didn't answer my question." Edith said, sitting down.

Felix pressed his lips and stood in front of the desk, avoiding her gaze. He blinked, feeling his eyes water.

"My sister passed away in a school fire, my mother passed away from grief shortly after, and my father was never to be seen again."

He's told no one about his family before. Everyone knew his grandfather and uncle but never dared to inquire about his immediate family. He remembered the look in his mother's eyes upon hearing about a fire that started in Lola's school.

"Oh, Felix. I'm so sorry. I shouldn't have asked."

"It's okay. It's all in the past. I was interning here when it happened and they were back home," he exhaled deeply. "...in Virginia." Edith typed in her password for Skype and stared at Felix. "If you're wondering how I earned my wealth," he continued. "That's a story for another day,"

"Okay," she responded.

"I'll leave you to it, then. If you need anything, I'll be downstairs doing my part and taking phone calls."

He turns and opens the door, giving Edith and the photos one last look before shutting the door. Edith heard him jogging down the stairs. She licked her lips. *Okay, you haven't worked from home in a while. This should be fun.*

Edith typed a message, sending it to her team.

Hello, all. I apologize for the tardiness. It's unlike me. I'm currently out of the office today; possibly tomorrow as well. I would like to congratulate our team for last week's efforts and wish to tackle more projects this week. I will be at my computer for inquiries on ideas and will answer questions that you may have.

The inbox received a notification.

Good morning, Ms. Rosu. This is Victoria, Mr. Radley's assistant. He's informed me you're working from home. In case you want to work remotely for a week or take a load off, I can forward any requests to your manager.

Edith sat and stared at the screen with her mouth ajar. *What do I say?* Her cheeks grew pink. She pressed her lips and typed.

Wonderful to meet you, Victoria. Thank you for the heads up, but I'll be back in the office shortly. The team appreciates my absence. I'll still give updates and keep everyone posted.

The inbox pings again.

Understood, Miss. Pleasure to meet you as well. I'll be here if you have questions for me or for Mr. Radley.

Edith stared at the polite reply. *She doesn't know about us, does she?*

Edith stared at the conversation then spent the next two hours accepting blueprint proposals and project pitch ideas. Downstairs, Felix had the TV on as he was watching a crime documentary. In three hours, Edith had to take her lunch as if she were in the building today.

Clicking through email and typing brief messages, encouraging her teammates were all she could do. She licked her lips and swallowed, switching her work status to break before walking out of the office. Edith crept down the stairs and made her way into the kitchen. Felix was in the living room in his recliner, holding the remote. He looked over at Edith, who turned the kitchen light on.

"Can I help you with something, Miss?" he asked playfully. Felix stood up from the recliner and walked up behind Edith, burying his face into her hair. "Someone's hungry,"

Edith cleared her throat while pouring a cup of apple cider. "I need food, Mr. Radley,"

Felix stepped back and turned to open the refrigerator. He pulled out a small tub of cream cheese and grabbed a bagel behind him.

"Knives are in the drawer and plates are above you." he said, handing the bagel and cream cheese.

"Thanks,"

He smirked and headed back to the recliner. Edith plopped the bagel slices into the toaster and waited. Felix never let guests into his home. His neighbors were just as busy and believed it was impolite to interrupt his personal time. The only person who spoke a word to him, was an elderly woman who took her nine-year-old poodle for walks.

As the Chief Executive Officer, Felix was in charge of over a hundred thousand people.

He knew that handling a community of people meant assertiveness and precision. He couldn't afford to make mistakes or take a second away from work unless it was an off day.

He was as charming as he was respectful to his peers and neighbors. They returned the same respect. Each person arrived to work with their own dreams and goals, and they transmute that passion into their work ethics.

Felix particularly admired and preferred to work closely with the engineering team for they weren't afraid to share their passion with everyone and hoped the company thrived.

He pulled out his phone and logged onto his laptop. Everyone assumed he had minimal work to do, but the managerial team and directors gave a string of tasks for him to complete every week.

This week, he scheduled to meet with investors and market analysts. A presentation awaited him on Thursday.

Edith listened to Felix's voice deepen and switch tone as he responded to requests from his team.

"I'm meeting Ben and Tracey in Quincy to gather information." he says, looking toward the kitchen. "Yes, sir. I'm delighted to hear from the others." his voice echoed. A light chuckle slipped out of his mouth, making Edith smile. "Thank you for the call, Mr. Henley. I'll speak to you again soon. Bye, now."

The call ended shortly.

Felix stretched and yawned. The toaster's ding made Edith jump. She took the butter knife and dipped it into the cream cheese tub, and dispersed it on her bagel. Edith put the butter knife to her lips and licked the cream cheese off. She put the bagel together and took a bite before making her way over to Felix, who shut his eyes and laid the recliner back.

"Sounds like you're a busy man." Edith said, smiling.

She held the bagel in her right hand and placed her left hand on Felix's chest. He took her hand, making her walk around the recliner. Edith sat on his lap. He cupped her face with his hand. His thumb glided on her bottom lip.

"Since you're on break, I want to keep you busy," he pulled his hand away and smiles with a gleam in his eye.

Edith bit into her bagel and giggled as Felix's lips touched hers. If she were to get the promotion, this is what Edith would have to work with; a meticulous, orderly boss with a persistent hunger for her.

10

Despite Victoria's message to Reginald, he wanted her at the office pronto. He was bold enough to send a lengthy email to Edith on Wednesday morning. Felix was unaware, making rounds for his business meetings.
In the most condescending way possible, he sent:

It has been brought to my attention that you have worked out of the office. Mr. Radley's assistant knows of your accomplishments. They are impressive, indeed. However, as your director, I request you to send the schedule and work changes to me and not the CEO. If this issue persists, you will be given a warning and notice will be sent to the HR.

Kind regards,
Reginald
Thomas Director

Edith blinked at the message, laughing inside her mind. She cursed under her breath. It's doubtful that Felix would fire Reggie for being demeaning, but it wasn't impossible.
Edith smiles, wanting to bite back. Felix has a hold on her. She took a deep breath. There was nothing wrong with working from home. Plenty of office workers have

done it. Edith felt she could stand up to her boss. She had already reassured Victoria that she'll be back at the office soon.

Edith sat back in the office chair, smiling at the phone screen. Her fingers glided across the keyboard.

Reginald,

I appreciate your concern. Although you won't have to worry about my job performance, Reggie. It'd be best if you worried about your own.

She bit her lip, reading her message word for word. The front door downstairs opened and squeaked. Felix closed the door after he entered and set his keys on the wall hook.

Edith swiftly discarded the message. She sat up straight and turned the chair around to face the door. She pretended to swipe and browse on her phone. The office door opened and Felix entered, grinning from ear to ear.

"Hey," he says.

"Felix!" she chuckles nervously. "You're home early."

Her eyes moved to his arm. Felix raised his hand out from behind his back, revealing a pink rose.

"This is for you," he said.

Edith takes the rose with glistening eyes.

"Oh, thank you." she moved, wanting to kiss him, but he turned to face the door.

"Are you hungry? Let's go out for a bite."

Edith's legs numbed at the words, let's go out. She licked her lips and swallowed. "I'm actually starving. You have perfect timing."

Felix chuckled as she giggled nervously.

He gestured for her to step out of the office, and he followed. They took their time to get ready, as it was only seven o'clock. I want to take her out to dinner. *She's worked hard enough today.*

Felix put on a baby blue dress shirt and gray slacks. He could feel Edith stare as he put his belt on. As much as he wanted to strip it all off and take her to bed, both of them agreed to fill their stomachs before doing anything. Edith smiles at her mask sitting on the dresser.

She pulled on an emerald green bodycon dress, feeling her curves. She paired the dress with diamond and gold earrings and a beige, cropped cardigan. Her hair was curled and flowed down to her shoulder in waves. She knew that this wasn't a date, but it didn't hurt to look good.

Edith stared at herself in the mirror, imagining Felix standing behind her. He was already slipping on his shoes and grabbing his jacket.

Felix didn't want to go through calling for a reservation, so they opted for a lavish French restaurant downtown that allowed walk-in guests. The server seated them rather quickly, blushing at Felix's friendly gaze.

Edith ordered a bottle of Moscato for the evening.

A moscato? Decent choice, Ms. Rosu; Felix thought.

"I hope you don't mind the occasion. I just wanted to thank you as your boss for working so hard." his eyes stared into hers. Edith's straight lips curved. Your boss. His words echoed in her mind. He wasn't exactly her boss, but she knew what he meant. "I'm excited about that promotion for you,"

"I'm trying my hardest, sir." Edith smiles, then lifted the menu up to her face. Calling him sir in a public place felt odd.

Felix already knew what he wanted to order, tapping his foot to shake the blood-rushing feeling and arousal between his legs. The server comes back with the bottle of wine, once again grinning at Felix's godly features.

"I'll be happy to take your orders now if you're ready."

"Wonderful," Felix says, keeping his eyes on the menu. "I'll have the Salmon l'Estragon."

"Perfect, and for you, Miss?" the server writes his order on the pad and looks over at Edith.

"Steak Frites, please. Thank you,"

Felix smiles at the way Edith pronounced the name and laid the napkin on his lap. The server left and Edith looked at Felix, taking her napkin and putting it on her lap as well. "I rarely go out to eat," she says. "I was always so busy with work and other things that I just resort to fast-food." her cheeks flushed.

"You should be able to treat yourself." Felix said. His eyes water. "We can go anywhere. Or I can cook for you,"

"You cook?"

"Of course I do. I don't exactly have the means to hire a personal chef." Felix chuckles.

Edith laughed along with him. Her eyes moved to a woman approaching their table. Her intimidating eyes met with Edith's and shifted to Felix.

"Felix. I don't believe it's you," she gasped. Her red lipstick was brighter than Edith's.

"Siobhan. Hi," he stood up and Siobhan reached to kiss him on the cheek. "I haven't seen you in ages."

Siobhan wore a tight plum-colored dress and light beige heels. She curled her hair and tied it into a ponytail. The color of her nails matched her burning hazel eyes. Her makeup was hardly noticeable except for the highlighter on her cheeks. She kept a small Yves Saint Laurent bag on her arm.

Felix sat back down, and Edith's lips kept straight. The other woman hovered, keeping her attention on him.

"I'm in town for a few days to see a friend who's in labor." Siobhan smiles with her seductive eyes. She tapped his arm playfully. "How are things with you?" her giggle sent a blow to Edith's stomach.

"I'm still the same old workaholic." he laughs lightly.

Siobhan looks at Edith again and grins at Felix.

"Well, it was lovely to see you again, Felix. I hope we can talk soon." she said. Siobhan pulled out a post-it sheet from her purse and a black pen as if she had prepared for this moment. She jotted down her phone number, kissed the sheet leaving a lipstick mark, and stuck it on the tablecloth. "Call me sometime," her wink made Edith shiver.

Felix took the note and put it inside his jacket.

"We'll talk soon, Siobhan." he smiles.

"Ciao, Felix."

11

Edith and Felix made it back to his house after dinner. She was silent and slipped her heels off without batting an eye at him. Felix's body language was tame. He was indifferent; no pull or desire for that woman. The beginning of December was near.

Edith kicked her heels off and carried them in one hand. She lazily walked up the stairs as Felix went to his recliner. She looked over at the exhausted CEO, imagining him sitting in a recliner well into his seventies. Edith pushed the bedroom door open and planted herself on the bed. She panted into the pillow, wanting to lie on her chest until she fell asleep.

What she actually thought of doing was screaming into the pillow. Felix is a handsome, wealthy, and conservative man. All eyes would be on him each day of his life. Edith was a beauty herself, although she didn't want to admit how many times men wanted to court her. For Felix, she was only a pet taken in by him through pity. Still, he was her hero.

She stared at Felix with doubt sitting in the back of her mind. Was Siobhan an ex-girlfriend? Were there others? Did he have contacts on his phone? Her luck with love was always short-lived; there was a kiss, a couple of dates, and no promise of the future. *My future is to become better than I was before. I owe it to myself.*

She sighed, tossing her purse onto the floor, and laid on her back with arms spread and legs stretched. She shook the idea of Felix flirting with women other than her. What was her place in his life, anyway? Edith stared unconsciously at the bedside table. Was there a reason Felix had asked her to live with him? He was already a self-sufficient man, doing anything and everything to keep himself afloat.

Edith was merely there to keep him company. Would he look after her, too?

Felix steps through the doorway, admiring Edith as she fell half-asleep. She squints her eyes.

"You're tired already?" he says, sitting on the edge of the bed. Edith turns to face him.

"Who was that woman at the restaurant?" she asked.

Felix smiles. "That woman was Siobhan. My colleague Walter used to run a mentorship program for beginner programmers. I met Siobhan at a conference he held." Edith looked up at him. He stared into her eyes and put a hand on her arm. "She's not my type." he laughed, knowing she was feeling solicitous. "What is your type?"

"My type is an ingenious and headstrong woman; someone who takes what she wants."

Edith's lips curved downward slightly.

I don't always know what I want.

Edith's eyes fell to her lap. His hint prompted her to sit up. Her dress rose for its purpose. Felix kept his hands on his lap, eager to see what Edith would do to him. She licked her bottom lip and placed her hands on his shoulders. He smiles furtively as she leaned closer to him. Her breasts pressed against him as he turned his head, awaiting the kiss.

She put her lips on his, inhaling and moaning impatiently. His lips pressed back vigorously. Felix now pulled her onto his lap and cradled her while they kissed passionately. Edith acknowledged the smell of his cologne. The man likes Gucci; she thought.

"It's too warm here," he said. Felix takes her hand. "Let's go downstairs."

Edith and Felix walked out of the room, and he closed the door behind her. He led her down the steps and pulled her up to his waist. Edith wrapped her legs around his waist and put her arms around his neck, reaching down his back for a proper grip. He continued kissing her softly, wanting to keep her arousal filled. She breathed and moaned from the shock sent by the kiss. He grins, bringing her to the dining table. The warmth from his hands transferred down Edith's legs.

Felix set Edith down on the table. She sat firmly as he stood in between her legs and relaxed her hands on the table. His lips crashed into hers repeatedly, sealing in her desire for him. While sticking his tongue inside her mouth, Felix brushed his hands up her hips and his fingers found the edges of her thong.

Edith kept her eyes shut, enjoying the feeling of his tongue colliding with hers. He pulls her thong down impatiently and groans. Felix rubbed Edith's inner thigh before leading his fingers to her center. The thought of being naughty on the table was new to Edith, but not unusual.

She accepted the idea of being fucked against it.

"I want you to be mine, Edith," Felix moaned in her mouth, giving her another reason to be wet.

"I'm already yours," she melted from his touch.

Edith groaned as Felix guided his fingers, rubbing the middle finger on the nub of her clitoris in a circular motion. "Ooh," she cooed.

"My minx likes to be touched, doesn't she?" he let out a low chuckle.

"Touch me, Mr. Radley." she moaned and gasped as he rubbed harder.

She enjoyed being a good little slut for him.

Edith lifted her dress up more. The cold air slapped against her thighs and slid under her bare ass. Felix wanted her to suffer and ache for him.

"Wait here," he whispered into her ear.

She nearly whimpered. *What's he doing?*

Felix walked over to the thermostat to set it to seventy-five degrees, muttering something about not wanting to freeze. He then walked into the laundry room and reached for a bin on the upper shelf.

"Close your eyes and turn around." he yelled out. Edith blinked at his request. "Do it." she licked her lips and faced the table, pressing her abdomen against the edge. Edith cleared her throat and closed her eyes. "Ready?" he called out.

"I'm ready." she replied. *Ready for what?*

Felix smiles slyly, slipping the blindfold into his pocket and holding the vibrator and anal beads in his hands. Although he sanitized the anal beads and egg vibrator, his mind flashed back when he used them on Siobhan; a secret that Edith can never know about.

Her inviting curves and teasing breasts warranted a ride home after the conference. Felix's colleague Philip thought it was so polite and heroic of him to offer rides home. Siobhan was another plaything for Felix, but Edith was different. He actually cared about her and wanted her protected at all costs. The kink was a just a bonus, a praise for her being an ambitious fuck doll.

He walked out of the laundry room with an aching bulge in his pants. His slacks felt tighter with his cock, restricting him. He turned his head and stared at Edith, who did as she was told. Her obedience pleased him. Days at the office would be euphoric if she were to work on his floor of the building.

He cleared his throat and deepened his voice to appear dominant.

"Are your eyes closed, Ms. Rosu?" Felix asked, knowing the answer. Edith's dress fell down to her knees.

Felix clicked his tongue at the sight and Edith opened her eyes. She wiggled her shoulder to shake off an itch. Realization struck her; Mr. Radley wanted to play. "Keep your eyes closed." he said in a low, seductive tone.

Felix placed the items on the end table nearby, keeping Edith waiting. He approached and stood behind her with the blindfold. "Are you ready to play, pet?" he whispered. Pet. She hadn't heard that name in weeks.

"Yes, sir."

He put his arms in front of her, blindfolding Edith and tying a knot at the back of her head.

"Sir?" he asked.

"Mr. Radley,"

Felix pressed one hand on her back and unzipped his pants with the other. Edith wiggled her hips. Do it, put it in! she thought. The lips of her sex became dry. Felix wrapped his hand around his cock and gave it a quick pump. He tapped the head of his cock on Edith's ass, teasing her crack.

"Felix, don't." she choked.

Spit slid down her throat.

He smiles to himself and backed away from her again. She groaned impatiently. His cock twitched at the sound. Felix grabbed the anal beads from the end table and put it in his mouth, lubricating each sphere. He didn't enjoy the metal taste, but needed to fit the beads in somehow.

Keeping the beads in his mouth, Felix stood behind Edith once again.

"Felix, please." she begged. "Felix?" he palmed her ass before sliding a finger against her crack. His touch made Edith shudder. He pushed a finger inside her hole and pumped gently, groaning. "Who am I, Ms. Rosu?"

"Mr. Radley," she moaned. *This is torture.*

To his surprise, Edith was enjoying the feel of his finger pumping in and out of her forbidden hole. It lubricated itself, making his job easier. Felix sucked lightly on the beads before teasing Edith and pushing them into her carefully.

"Oh," Edith gasped. Her cheeks burned up.

"That's right, pet. I have a toy for you," Felix said, watching the beads enter. He smacked her ass cheek, and she felt a slight pinch. Felix held his cock and rubbed it against Edith's pussy lips. "Looks like my minx is hungry," he whispered.

With that, he stuck the head of his cock inside her and pushed. The buildup inside Edith popped out a gush of cum. Felix smacked her ass until the cheeks turned pink. She moaned and groaned, wanting to grab onto something. Edith surrendered to his control, stretching her arms on the table and resting her head. Felix listened as she whimpered and moaned quietly. He twisted the anal beads, moving them in and out.

"You can do better than that, pet. Moan for me."

Felix thrust harder, moving the beads at his cock's pace. Edith never imagined being double-penetrated by two men. She wouldn't have to; this was doing enough. She squealed and moaned at his command, focusing her attention on the tingling sensation the beads gave. Felix slowed down and thrust with all his might. "That's a good girl," he swept her hair aside and gave a hard spank.

Edith felt the heat and shivered down to her ankles. Felix enjoyed how beautiful she looked while being taken in a dress. He lifted the hem slightly and smacked her ass cheeks one more time.

"Oh fuck," she squealed.

A thought slid into Felix's mind intrusively.

"Tell me, Ms. Rosu," he whispered into her ear aggressively, thrusting harder. "Were you jealous of Siobhan?" *What? No way!* Her mind shouted. He continued to thrust. "You can tell me. I'm not mad," he breathed, giving another hard spank.

"No, sir. I'm not jealous." she whined.

"Hmm?" he asked, curving his eyebrows.

Where was he going with this?

He rested the palm of his hand on her ass, itching to smack it again.

"I wasn't jealous of her," Edith exhaled. "Mr. Radley, please. Fuck me more. Don't stop," she begged.

He twisted the beads and pulled them out. Edith felt a part of her being taken away. He pumped faster, causing her legs to shake along with the table. Spurts of his semen released inside her. Edith whimpered some more, feeling her cum spill.

12

Edith crossed her arms, staring at the clothes rack, and finally deciding on a pink silk lingerie. *This guy makes hell of a lot more money than me.* Shouldn't he be living in a mansion with extra rooms and closets? She pulled her hair over her shoulder and Felix scanned her body from head to toe. Edith sighed, noting the limited space she had for her clothes while the pampered CEO had a full closet to himself.

His bedroom was fairly large enough for two queen-sized beds. Edith licked her lips and pulled the lingerie onto her body while Felix slipped on a fresh pair of boxers. He laid on the bed with an arm underneath his head.

Edith crawled onto the bed next to him and sighed gratefully.

She propped herself up, leaning against the pillow and watched Felix. Mr. Radley looks like such an angel. He blinked up at her and stretched his arm across her waist. He grazed his fingers onto her lingerie's fabric then pressed onto Edith's side, making her gasp. Felix glances at her pert breasts. He moved his eyes to her lips and briskly planted a kiss. Edith exhaled through her nose, wanting to slip her tongue into his mouth but her mind pushed away the thought. She pressed on Felix's chest lightly for him to stop.

"I was wondering," she said. How do I ask this? The pompous manager was already tallying Edith's failures. She leaned on her elbow. Why isn't Felix being questioned? This slip up can be forgiven, I'm sure. Felix called the shots and did whatever he pleased. She envied the immediate acceptance to take an off-day even when it was with her.

"Hmm?" he turned his focus on her and breathed. She stared into his eyes and rubbed the itch under her lip.

"Since you're the CEO, why aren't you at the office? HR would have placed me on a WANTED list."

He cracked a smile, caressing the top of her hand. *I wanted to spend time with you. Is that too much to ask?* he thought.

"I highly doubt they would do that to you. In part, I'm ensuring everything runs smoothly and trust you all to know what to do for the greater good of the company." he pressed his lips together then curved a smile. "If you prefer, you can continue remote work. I can handle the objections."

Edith looked away to hide her discomfort.

If Felix had high demands, how could she possibly work as a director to make someone like him happy?

She tapped deep within her thoughts, feeling her heart thud. I don't think I've seen critical reviews about this man yet. *The switch could flip and he might want to remove me from the company too. I've worked way too hard to go down like this.*

He watched her cheeks flush. She sighed and stared at the ceiling. "Edith" he says. She had a dead look in her eyes. *None of this should have happened.* She pictured his hands on her hips as she stood behind his desk. Edith blinked the thought away. *Nothing good would come out of sleeping with the boss. He'll leave me.* A tear slid down her right cheek at the thought of him breaking her heart. , he shouts in her head.

"Edith, look at me," he breathed. The ruffles in his hair gave a boyish look. She gazed into his eyes. "If you get promoted next month, I won't turn into the demeaning evil boss people imagine one to be." he gave an earnest look. *How did you—* Her eyes moved slightly to look at him. "I'll spare you if that happens." This made Edith giggle as her tears dried. Felix removed his arm, allowing Edith to pull the covers up to her chest. She sighed in relief and laughed to herself. "How would you feel if I got promoted?" Felix cleared his throat, smiling briefly.

How would I feel? I'd feel relieved! Ecstatic.

"It would please me to have you around. You'd stimulate me," he said, catching Edith's expression as she opened her mouth. "Not just in that way. I want to see how well you'd do as a director. Your success is as important as mine." he moved closer, breathing lightly and whispering into her ear. "If that's what you want, you'd also have more play-time with me."

Edith blushed at the word play-time. She playfully shoved Felix and he chuckled.

"We'd work well together, Edith." he continued. "Think about it, working with me will lift the stress off your shoulders and it would mean the world to me."

She slumped back down, pressing her head onto the pillow and Felix also laid back. Edith pictured herself having an office right across his; frequently visiting, giving reports, and having him embrace her mid-sentence. It felt like a dream. Anyone else couldn't crush this dream.

Felix closed his eyes and reminisced about the past for a moment. My life is changing. This could be the start of something new for me. When he was a young man, Felix was left with many responsibilities. He's not like Edith at all. His family was insistent on discipline and keeping the family name. Business was business to the Radley household. There was no time for distraction.

Brighton Technologies was a billion dollar company and Felix was less than that. His grandfather had loaned him a hundred grand to start a small business, a small tech store in Massachusetts.

Later, he found out that his family founded the company.

Carrying on the family business wasn't something he wanted to do, but he chose to. Felix was on good terms with his uncle and grandfather. Passing up the opportunity would have placed him as a tech seller instead of an innovator.

He would sit in his office and curse after shifts, staring at emails and checking blueprints, feeling like a burden to the men in his family. Despite the rising stats and impressionable numbers, none of this was good for him. Edith helped him realize. No other woman he's met saw him the way she did. No one cared to ask about his past.

Edith turned to face the closet door. Felix snuggled close, with his nose buried in her hair as he spooned her. "I don't want you to think ahead of yourself so much." he kissed her shoulder. "Relax, enjoy your weeks as manager, and we'll see where your career goes."

"What about my peers?" she turned her head as he breathed down her neck. "I'd want one of them to work with me too," Edith dropped her shoulders, frowning to herself. *You can't have your cake and eat it too, Edith. Slow down.*

"Then you can have a co-manager." *I need her to be solo, but how can I say no? What is she thinking?* Felix thought. "Although I'd like for us to work together, a directorial position is no easy feat and I'm sure you'll need guidance. I want to make things easier for you. For us."

You're playing with fire, Ms. Rosu.

If he were her mentor, Felix could help Edith become the best version of herself. He wanted to grow closer to her.

Edith sat quietly on the edge of the bed with the computer on her lap. She stared dryly at the new message in front of her. This time it was from Sally, from HR. She asked Edith to forward her schedule to her as soon as possible.
Edith squinted her half-shut eyes at the computer screen.
Felix knocked on the door lightly.

"Come in," she said. The blue light from the screen reflected in her eyes.

"Don't you want to eat?"

Felix asked, entering the room. His eyes flickered at the computer screen. "What's that?"

"Reginald was upset about taking days out of the office, and now someone from human resources sent me a message." Edith looked up at him.

He moved closer to see the screen and furrowed his brows.

"They might be doing their jobs, but this is unacceptable. I have allowed people to work from home before. Each manager should know it's permitted." Felix moved to kiss Edith on the cheek. "Do you want me to do something about this?"

"If you interfere, they might figure something out about us." Edith replied, signing out of the email.

"Then I'll have the VP talk to them or perhaps someone from the directors' floor. Speaking of which, I'll put in a referral to the board to consider your promotion."

"You'd do that for me?"

"Of course,"

Edith walked over to place the laptop on the armchair nearby. Felix stared as she laid back in bed and fluffed her pillow. *He'd do anything for me. I can trust him.* She placed a hand on her stomach, feeling the queasiness subside. Felix allowed her to lie on his chest and she stretched her arm across his waist. Edith let out a grateful sigh.

"I'm always here for you," Felix whispered with a smile. "...as your boss, of course."

"You know you'd be more than just my boss," she blinked her eyes at him. Felix smirked and leaned down to kiss her lips. She licked her lips to savor his taste.

"Edith I—" Felix paused, closing his mouth; panic set in his eyes. Should he tell her? Will he tell her? His palms sweat as her stare burned through his guilt. *I like you, Edith. You're worth so much more.* "I'll do whatever I can to keep our 'business' between us." he put air quotes around business. His words tugged a string in her heart.

Edith couldn't possibly keep these feelings bottled up for long.

Growing up, her mother had always taught her to be headstrong yet listen to her own heart. It was always better to say how you'd feel than say nothing at all. But I want him to confess first; she thought. *I don't want to make a fool of myself.*

Does he like her as a subordinate or something more? She couldn't detect the tone in his voice. As she observed his heartbeat, feeling his chest rise and fall, Edith's cheeks flushed and her heart pounded. I'll be patient. I won't give up on him. She cuddled closer to him, taking in his warmth. He kissed her temple and cleared his throat before falling asleep. Edith stared at his face before turning in for the night.

13

Felix left his office to grab sheets of paper from the copy machine. Edith sat in the guest seat looking at the palms of her hands as they reddened from her anxiety. Felix returned, looking directly at the panic in her eyes.

He cleared his throat.

"Don't worry, the floor is empty right now." This was a side of her that Felix never thought to see but he did his best to keep calm. He wrapped his arms around her, smiling at their height difference.

She sighed, forgetting that anyone could knock on the door and interrupt them. Her body shivered. Felix released her from his embrace. "You're okay, Edith." he whispered. He sat on the edge of his desk and stared at the woman in front of him. Edith exhaled again, standing up and placing her hands on her hips.

Felix paused for a moment, grimacing at the thought of Bianca breathing down his neck. She was twenty-seven with the mindset of a twenty-one-year-old party girl. Bianca clearly wasn't his type. He glued his eyes onto the outline of Edith's heart-shaped face. *You shouldn't be sighing so much.*

"I've been thinking, Edith." he mentions. She turned, noticing his stare. She looked away, feeling the heat in her cheeks. *Why is he staring at me?* she thought. Does Felix like me? "We'll keep our relationship secret." *But what kind of relationship is this, Mr. Radley?*

"You're eating me alive, Felix," she replies with a nervous laugh.

"I'm pretty sure I'm full."

Felix walked over to his desk and logged in. No one contacted him within the last week. His mind shifted to Bianca.

For Bianca to say that she fucked a man in a higher job position was one thing. She enjoyed the gloating and seeing Edith knock down a notch. Felix made it certain that he wanted Edith to work with him, to be his partner in more ways than one, not this overachiever.

The board members may agree that failing to notify the directorial team and especially the CEO of company changes would cause a warning but they could shrug a promotional decision. The upper management wouldn't give a damn about a leveled up employee.

"Do you want me to have a talk with Kyle? Or should I speak with Bianca instead?" he asked, looking down at the floor.

Edith broke away from her thoughts.

"What?" her hair draped over her shoulder. Her widening eyes caused Felix to rest his expression. "You shouldn't speak to either of them." she continued. "I'm the only one who knows about this and Bianca's a chatterbox. Things could backfire."

Felix smiles again. Take it easy. It was just a suggestion.

"Okay. Well, you're her manager. What do you suggest we do, Ms. Rosu?" he stared at her, teasing out an answer. Pressure weighed on her shoulders now.

"I'll have a talk with Kyle to discuss updates on the promotion. If he acts shady, then you can have a chat with him. Bianca wants to play a game and I won't be a participant."

Felix walked over to the door and checked the lock. He pulled the window blinds down and glanced at Edith, scanning her body from top to bottom.

"This sounds like quite the dilemma. I can always fire her." he laughed.

Felix turned to Edith, unable to contain the aching bulge that grew in his slacks. He dipped a hand in his pocket to adjust his underwear.

"Do you want me to have a talk with Kyle? Or should I speak with Bianca instead?" he asked, looking down at the floor.

Edith broke away from her thoughts.

"What?" her hair draped over her shoulder. Her widening eyes caused Felix to rest his expression. "You shouldn't speak to either of them." she continued. "I'm the only one who knows about this and Bianca's a chatterbox. Things could backfire."

Felix smiles again. *Take it easy. It was just a suggestion.*

"Okay. Well, you're her manager. What do you suggest we do, Ms. Rosu?" he stared at her, teasing out an answer. Pressure weighed on her shoulders now.

"I'll have a talk with Kyle to discuss updates on the promotion. If he acts shady, then you can have a chat with him. Bianca wants to play a game and I won't be a participant."

Felix walked over to the door and checked the lock. He pulled the window blinds down and glanced at Edith, scanning her body from top to bottom.

"This sounds like quite the dilemma. I can always fire her." he laughed.

Felix turned to Edith, unable to contain the aching bulge that grew in his slacks. He dipped a hand in his pocket to adjust his underwear.

"I don't want Bianca gone. I just want her to calm down. I've waited years to get this job position and I deserve some betterment."

Felix muted Bianca and job in his mind. *We can afford to lose her. I need you now, Ms. Rosu.* He placed a palm on the desk and gestured Edith to come to him. She looked into his eyes and stepped in between his legs. He put his arms around her, burying his face in her hair. Her tugged onto the skirt of her emerald green velvet dress, pulling it up. Edith put her hand on his, wanting him to stop. "I'm only here to talk to you. We can't do anything right now. Felix, please,"

Felix blocked the door, standing in front of Edith. He turned the lock and pulled the blinds down. He stared, admiring her petite figure. This is awfully familiar; she thought, biting her lip. The familiar pinch of arousal makes itself known to her. He sensed her pheromones and looked down at her lips. *Someone's excited for me.*

"All I heard was 'Please fuck me, Felix'." he smiles mischievously, letting out a small groan as his pants tightened. "Tell you what, why don't we play our own game?" he lowered his voice. "We'll let Bianca brag about her promising advancement, but in the end, I want you to have it. I want you to be my little office minx." he breathed into her ear as his hand moved up further underneath the dress. "Nice thong, Ms. Rosu,"

All Edith could do was whimper at his touch.

Felix's rough hands glided up her inner thigh, and he planted his lips on the right side of her neck. A whiff of sweet Yves Saint Laurent surely seduced him. Edith's fate in this company was in his hands. Felix could order them to give her the promotion or implement it himself. He couldn't wait to watch her succeed and bury himself inside her.

With a swift grab, Edith has her back against the desk. She groaned looking at his waist as his bulge grew. Felix had no choice but to tame himself and give her momentary satisfaction. Behind the wall, voices of men echoed. Edith mouthed the word *fuck*.

Felix quickened his thrusts before pulling out and fastening his belt. Edith fingered through her hair and covered her face, sneaking behind him as he opened the door.

She quietly sauntered toward the direction of the elevator without glancing back. Upon exiting his office, Felix noticed Kyle speaking with another man, furrowing his brows. Felix pulled onto the doorknob, shutting the door quietly.

The older man Kyle was speaking to whispered something in his ear and patted him on the back.

"I'll see you tomorrow, Kyle!"

"Looking forward to it, Victor!" he waved and turned around, exchanging glances with Felix. Kyle waved. "Felix, buddy! What's up?"

"I'm just ending my day. Hey Kyle, I was meaning to talk to you."

Felix flashed a smile.

"What is it?"

Felix looked around and walked over to an empty desk. He sat down in a chair and Kyle followed.

"There's some news about the promotion being advanced by two weeks. It might be gossip, but do you know about this?"

Kyle rubbed the back of his head.

"Oh! Yeah, I talked with some of the board members the other day and I think we can agree on these candidates."

His smile dropped, as did Felix's.

"What do you mean?"

Kyle sat in the seat next to Felix, slouching and putting his arms behind his head casually.

"I've seen the top five runners. Albert, Bianca, Wes, Morgan, and for some reason, Edith." he snickered. *I don't like your tone*, Felix thought.

"What's wrong with Edith?"

"The managerial team doesn't like her that much. There were only two people who did and they left to work at another company years ago."

Felix balled his hand into a fist.

"Who do you think would be a good fit as a director then?"

"Don't tell anyone just yet, but Bianca would do a fine job as a director. She has a track record as senior research engineer. Also, that beauty can bounce." Kyle's dazed look changed and his mouth gaped open. "I mean she worked just as long as Edith and deserves something better than what she has." Kyle sat up and waited for Felix's response.

Edith's going to be even more disappointed. Felix sighed. *She'll still have me, regardless.*

"Edith is Bianca's superior. She knows what's best for the team and the company." Felix countered. Kyle discreetly rolled his eyes. "Since I can't change the two-week window, I'll think of something for this week and have results by then."

"Okay, then that's settled." Kyle smirked. "Just shoot me an email and we'll talk, and give Dalton the results as well."

"Not a problem," It's a major problem, Felix thought. He pressed his lips into a straight line as he watched Kyle walk away.

On the ride home, Felix envisioned Edith's lips curve into a frown at the news. Her eyes watered as she looked at him. He held her hands on his lap and leaned in for a soothing kiss. Her salary wasn't awful, but this was about her pride and joy of being at Brighton. If she hadn't moved in with him, Edith would still live in the small three-bedroom home alone, bitter, and sexless.

Back at home, Felix poured himself a cup of Jasmine tea to drink after his meal. Edith was in the kitchen. She wiped the counter and pressed a button to start the dishwasher. Felix sipped his tea as she walked over to sit at the table with him.

"I have to admit, work has been real tough on me lately." Edith sighed, folding her hands together.

"Was it like this before we met?" his voice cracked at the word *we*.

Five years into this job was hell. The workload is a pain. She would have spoken up if it weren't for the strict labor laws.

Edith gave him a blank stare before opening her mouth to speak. "I'm relieved to know that you exist, and quite frankly, I'm glad to know that you run the company, and not some deranged maniac." Felix nearly spit out his drink and laughed. His pearl white teeth glistened under the light above them. "It's true," she continued. A tiny smirk appeared. "I'm grateful for the opportunities I have at this job,"

Edith removed the hair-tie from her wrist and proceeded to wrap her hair into a messy bun. Felix drank the tea halfway, gulping and savoring the taste as he closed his eyes. "Would you still want to be with me if you didn't get promoted? What are your plans?" Edith felt uneasy.

Would you stay... with me?

They glanced at each other as if they shared the same thought. She turned to him as he stood up from the table holding the empty tea cup.

"If the management wants to keep me, I'll stay." The turn of events squeezed the motivation out of her heart. "But if they give me more shit, then I'll be happy to leave for something better."

"Hmm," he says, washing the cup down with soap. "And your plans with me?"

You're the most caring and intoxicating man, I've met, Mr. Radley.

"I'd like to take things slow," *I don't know what we are.* "You're a great man, Felix. But I'm merely just an associate. I know nothing about you,"

"Then get to know me, Edith. You're more valuable than an associate. I want you to be mine."

Edith's heart skipped a beat as Felix placed his hand on her arm. She wouldn't be in his bed if she were just a fling. He would've told her to sleep on the recliner. Felix couldn't do that to her.

She was hooked onto his heart.

14

Felix entered the conference room, thinking about how time flew by. He sat in at the end of the table, listening to people chatter about plans with friends and family before it was time for discussion on the company's agenda for next quarter.

The holidays were approaching and he didn't want to spend the days alone. He sighed, unsure if Edith wanted to spend time with him despite their living arrangements.

He groaned in his hands. *I can't make her stay with me for Thanksgiving. What if she rejects me?* All Felix knew was that Edith lived alone and most likely didn't have friends here in Massachusetts. He was essentially all she had.

Randall from HR, Sonia from the board, three managers, and two of the directors entered the room. Sonia cleared her throat and straightened her dress shirt. Felix noticed her newly dyed bob cut and smirked to be polite.

Randall rolled his chair out to sit down, breaking Felix's train of thought.

"Felix," he says. "I've spoken to Sarah and the others. We've consulted with the CFO and the treasurer." he swallowed. "Our stats aren't looking good and some of the staff have underperformed this year."

Felix curved his brows, staring at the table to think. He'd almost forgotten the responsibilities he had before meeting Edith. Felix wondered if her position was affected.

"People are unhappy with customer service and the quality of our products, sir." Randall folded his hands, feeling the heat build in his palms.

Felix lowered his voice to sound intimidating.

"Have you checked with the engineering team? What about the product manager?"

"I've spoken to Adrianna about the matter and she's referred me to Edith,"

Felix's heart leapt. Edith had no problem directing her team and guiding them with proposals and blueprints so what's the problem?

"Well, what's the update?" he licked his lips and swallowed.

"We believe the submissions aren't up to par," Randall whispered but he was loud enough for the others to take notes on his words.

"What did the IT department have to say about this?" "I haven't heard back from them yet, but I don't believe some employees are playing their part, sir."

Felix wrote things down on the notepad in front of him and exhaled. "Very well."

For the next twenty minutes, Felix couldn't help but think Edith wasn't excelling at her job as he thought she would. What if she was just using him to gain a step up at the company? He clenched his fist and breathed, trying to block his doubt and listen to what the others had to report. New hires would mean dropping more cash on employees and accounting for their pay.

Kyle admitted to fucking a subordinate. Why not fire him?

Felix eased his posture in the seat. One of the managers kept his eyes on Felix like a hawk. Felix tried to fake a smile in the next five minutes.

Felix kept to himself for most of the day. He discovered the list of employees being hired.

There was also a list of people added in preparation for a layoff of underperforming individuals. Layoffs and firing were the hardest part of his job, but the HR and board of directors assisted with keeping the best performers. He sat in his office and poured half a glass of whiskey.

Having alcohol in the office wasn't a reccurring thing but he needed something other than coffee to clear his mind and soothe his heart. When speaking with Edith, he noticed the twitch of her bottom lip, the ache in her eyes, and heard the fear in her voice. We can be a lot closer if you would just trust me, Edith. He sighed, putting the cup down. Running a company was stress-inducing and no different from being the principal or dean of a school. Felix shook his head at the idea of Edith being a lovesick schoolgirl. She wasn't under his level; they met eye to eye. He requested to see Edith's file from someone at the human resources office. Within twelve minutes, Xavier emails the PDF file.

Felix has seen this information once or twice before, but back then, he didn't think of Edith as anything more than an associate; a smart one at that. Before he decided to pursue her, Felix never cared for a relationship. A majority of people who knew him dated plenty of times in their twenties and their experiences disinterested him. Felix felt that work was his first and only love.

Felix walked over and placed the empty cup next to the coffee machine and tucked the bottle of whiskey underneath his desk. She lives in your house man; he thought to himself. You're basically roommates. "I like my roommate," Felix muttered. He licked his lips and turned off the office light before exiting.

The drive home was silent. Fewer cars passed by today compared to the beginning of the week. It must have been normal for people to stay off the street during Thursdays. He arrived home two hours before Edith's shift would end.

Felix sat in his recliner, regretting not taking that bottle of whiskey home, and rummaged the kitchen for a bottle of champagne. Felix wasn't used to having such a close partnership with anyone. No one offered him help or guidance other than mentors in college. Once the operations began, Felix was forever alone.

If I treat Edith to be less than me, she'll never set foot here again; he groaned, massaging the bridge of his nose. He turned the TV on and flipped the channel to a movie. *Maybe being with her is a mistake.* The alcohol began to course through his veins, prompting his muscles to relax as he laid back into the recliner.

All Felix could think about was Edith deserving better, being with someone who's better. Though his heart couldn't let her go.

15

Bianca sat up straight with a smirk on her face, stacking papers on her desk. Her expression dropped when looking down the aisle towards Edith's office. *Soon, I'll have an office and I'll be making orders around here.* To her, being at the top was all that mattered. She hardly considered Edith as a friend and everyone knew Edith had her moments as the snarky boss.

Bianca had been dying to be in her shoes.

She remembered the eye-fucking Edith and Felix shared in the conference room. The dominance in his eyes was something Bianca craved from a man.

Edith reviewed the documents emailed by a few engineers. Bianca had sent her a lengthy essay detailing research for the upcoming at-home AI assistant robot that the company took two years to plan for. She only had time for the summary.

Edith took a breath and internally read the text.

The following information is for our next project "Milo". Milo is an efficient cellphone-sized robot AI wired to ensure customer satisfaction. It will be there at every beck and call, see the customer as its rightful owner, and listen to their every command.

This little robot will be there to fulfill their owner's needs.

Underneath her description was a signature line for Felix's approval. Was she going to submit this to Felix to get her praise? It has to be stamped by me first; she scoffed.

"I think I'm going to be sick," Edith muttered.

While reading the product description, Edith's chest tightened, and her palms sweat. *What if Bianca is toying with me?* Bianca's sudden infatuation with Felix flushed Edith's cheeks with fury. He doesn't want you; he wants me.

Edith pulled out her phone and texted Felix. This was all getting to her head. The switch to her critical thinking shattered.

Felix, I wanted to know. Is there an update regarding the VP situation?

There is.

That's great. Can we talk in your office today?

Can't. I'll be out for lunch to meet with someone.

Edith's lips curved. He must have a date. It could be Bianca or someone else Edith couldn't compete with.

Oh. Can we talk tonight?

I'll think about it. I have to go.

Her mind thought of many women walking out of his office day by day, gasping with satisfied grins on their faces. Felix followed them with his shirt undone and his chest had red lipstick marks, similar to the shade Edith wore.

It wasn't like that at all. Felix created this company, but he never thought he'd hire such monsters. If it had to lead to competition, the game would be two against two and Felix couldn't let Bianca, Kyle, or anyone else destroy Edith's confidence.

Edith spent the next hours contemplating what to say. She finished the last proposals and blueprint demands for the day and snuck out of her office. Hannah smiles shyly as Edith walked past her desk without a glance.

Edith excused herself early and drove home with her lips pressed together. Felix opened the front door with the phone in his hand. He watched Edith enter. She set her purse on the recliner. Felix stood behind Edith and rubbed her shoulders.

"Did you still want to talk?" She turned around, glancing at his lips.

"I had this crazy idea in my head that Bianca wants to come after you," she said, biting her bottom lip. Felix moved to the other recliner seat. Edith put her purse aside and sat on his lap.

"She won't have a chance because I'm not interested in her." he chuckled, wrapping his arms around Edith's waist. "I like you, Edith." her cheeks flushed. He likes her. This was something she didn't think he'd say out loud. "I trust that you'll have a bright future with your career."

"Do you like me as a colleague? Or something more?" she ran her finger over his chest, not knowing how aroused this made him feel.

Felix stared back into her eyes. *Where is this coming from?* He kept his hands on her hips. His neck muscles strained.

"I might like you more than I should." he replied with a straight face. *Trust me, I think I'm in love with you. Being in love isn't easy.* He watched as her eyes watered. *Talk to me, Edith.* She noticed the color of his eyes, a gold tint in pools of honey brown. Felix sat up straight.

Edith prepared to remove herself from his lap. He held her in place. Felix kept Edith in his arms and planted a soft kiss on her lips, causing her to moan.

There's no way I'm letting that other woman come near me, Felix thought. "Edith," he says, attempting to change the topic. "You know I can only respect Bianca as an employee." she listened intently. "As with you, it doesn't matter what you are to me because, as I've mentioned once, I like you, Edith. You have nothing to worry about regarding her." His voice went dry in a harsh tone. Felix's palms twitched.

Edith got up from Felix's lap and stared at him dead in the eye. *Wait.* "It doesn't matter what I am to you? So, what am I, Felix? Your fucktoy?" She crossed her arms and blinked irritably at the floor.

"Edith," he looked up at her, softening his gaze. "You are more than just a fucktoy," he took a deep breath. Edith crossed her arms and curved her eyebrows. "I don't know how I feel about you just yet, but when I look at you, I can tell you're the only woman I want. No one else,"

The line between like and love thickened. Lust was his shadow, but he wanted to tame it for her sake.

Edith straightened her posture and stared at the man for as long as she could. She liked him, too. She imagined the meter of her admiration freezing in the middle. What can she use to break the ice? Felix was an attractive man, and his lust sealed her in his grasp. But could there be something more? Felix wasn't ready for a commitment yet. He wanted more time.

"I would never intend to hurt you. I can't do that," he continued, taking her hand. Edith sat back on his lap. "Why don't we focus on your career for now?"

Edith touched her chin, and Felix brushed his hand over her face. He gently placed his lips on hers and looked into her eyes. This made Edith wish she didn't have to work so hard. She wanted Felix to hold and keep her in his arms.

"We can do that."

The day off arrived faster than the two had expected. Felix set the coffee machine to brew. He was up since four in the morning, thinking about how today would go. At least this time, both he and Edith caught a break. Edith tied the robe around her waist and entered the kitchen, yawning.

"What time is it?" she blinked.

"It's seven o'clock, but I want us to do something today."

"This early?" she squinted at the full cup he handed to her.

"I want to take you out today. There's a conference I'd like you to watch." he smiles, noticing her lips twitch into a frown. "You'll enjoy it. Trust me."

Edith stared at her drink and lifted it to her lips. A hint of sugar greeted her tongue. She tugged on her sleeve, sniffing the robe.

"Shower. I've already cleaned up an hour ago."

Edith got up from the table and excused herself. Felix lowered his eyes at her ass before walking over to the sink.

She entered Felix's bedroom. Edith pulled out a semi-formal dress and her undergarments. It was a simple black bodycon dress. She grew tired of trudging around in heels so midnight blue pointed flats would be perfect to wear until noon.

Winter was weeks away, and she hoped the water's temperature was hot enough. Her mind lingered on the upcoming days.

Both Felix and Edith expected the promotion announcement. This was one reason Felix couldn't sleep last night. Inside the shower, she inhaled the steam and ran her hands down her locks. The warm water splashed onto Edith's skin.

The bedroom door opened and Felix hummed the beginning of *I Just Called To Say I Love You* by Stevie Wonder. He sang as he slipped into a fresh pair of dress pants and pulled on the sleeves of his button-down shirt. He lifted his phone to check for the time, then looked at the bed.

He clicked his tongue and grabbed the pillows, stripped the pillow cases off, and gathered the comforter and sheets. He carried them in one arm and jogged downstairs to the laundry room. By the time he tossed linen into the washer washer, Edith finished drying her hair and got dressed.

She laid her jewelry on top of the dresser and applied her matte lipstick, looking into the mirror. Felix ran back up the stairs after starting up the washing machine. He walked in on Edith, putting her earrings on. Beautiful. He entered the room, meeting her eyes. Felix took Edith's gold necklace and stood behind her.

"May I?" he pushed her hair aside. The ends curled. She watched as he wrapped the gold chain around and locked it in place. It paired well with her small gold hoops.

They prepared to leave and drove across the water to a conference hall known to announce significant technology events for all to see. Edith gasped at the height of the building.

Felix smiles, putting a hand on her back, and crossed the street with her.

He sighed pleasantly, going up the steps and letting Edith walk in front of him. He opened the door for her and smiles.

"After you,"

16

The moment of truth was fast-approaching. Edith sat silently in her office, waiting for the green light from Felix. Her fingers glided across the keyboard. Her heart and mind weren't in sync. She logged out of the computer and sat back in her chair. This is ridiculous. I know the promotion is mine; she thought. Leaning forward, Edith tapped her fingers on the desk. *This is something Blanca would do.*

Hey, Felix texted. *I have good and bad news.*

We can talk in my office, or I can come to you.

For today, we should be careful. I want to keep a distance in case someone might see us.

Okay.

Felix exhaled. *Okay?* His heart sank. I don't know how much longer I can keep this up; he thought. He glanced at the clock.

We have an hour before the announcement. We can talk in Room 302B.

Being a foot away from Edith made Felix sexually frustrated. Tame your demons. He stood up from the desk and straightened his tie and picked up the phone, sending Edith a final message.

Let's meet right now.

Edith arrived at the conference room, waiting for Felix to enter first. He unlocked the door and entered, taking his place at the end of the table. Felix cleared his throat. Edith sat on the chair to his left. She smiles, playfully pretending to scoot away from him. He inhaled and grabbed the chair, pulling her closer.

"Now's not the time for games, Ms. Rosu," he said sternly. She gulped and sat still.

"So, what news do you have for me, Mr. Radley?" she put on her managerial tone.

He folded his hands and placed them on the table.

"I know you must be nervous about the results, but Declan has given me the list. I'm nervous too." he leaned down and pulled out a manila envelope from his briefcase.

"Are you going to allow me to see the list?"

"No, that's what sucks about this. I don't know the results either but," he paused, taking her hand. "Remember that I'm here for you." he looked into her eyes and took a double take at her breasts. *Fuck me.*

His mind blanked, and he sat back, faking a cough. Edith looked down at her shirt and buttoned all the way.

"Was there anything else, Mr. Radley?" her voice was soft, almost seductive, but she didn't mean it.

"Nothing changes if you won't move up a position, but there could be a follow-up discussion on this if necessary." He licked his bottom lip. "Of course, if you decide to leave, then that's fine by me."

"I see," she looked down at her hands. "What's the good news?"

The good news? Oh, yeah. Edith, I'm in love—shit. Do you really have to pulse right now? Felix took a breath and looked down at his crotch.

Edith tapped her foot lightly and Felix did the same, bouncing his leg to ease the growing ache in his slacks. Both of them wanted to be wild and free right now. *I need to have him; she thought. Felix knitted his eyebrows, trying to divert his attention somewhere else.

We can't.

"The good news," he paused and stared into her eyes. "The good news is that there are other open positions you can apply for in three months if you're unhappy with what you have now." He let out a nervous chuckle.

Edith's heart palpitated seeing the corners of Felix's lips move down. *If she leaves, this may be goodbye. If she applies to another position, who knows how they'd treat her again.*

He stood up from the table, packed his briefcase, and fixed his tie. He pulled the door open and bumped into someone's shoulder. "Oh! Excuse me," he looked up. "Kyle? What are you doing here?"

Shit! Shit! Shit!

Edith closed the door behind her. Her knees weakened. It wasn't like she did anything with Felix.

Kyle took a quick look at her and glared with suspicion. "I just needed to speak with someone on this floor. What are you two doing here?" he motioned. *Are you together?* He shook his head. *Nah, they can't be.*

"Edith and I are working together," he says, looking at her. "On a new project for next quarter. She just wanted to consult me about it."

"Hmm," Kyle curved his brows. "Well, I'll be seeing you later for the announcement, and you as well, Ms. Rosu." he exchanged a last look.

"Yep," Felix replied. "We'll see you there." *The suspense is killing me.*

He turned to Edith, who looked at him curiously. Kyle nodded at them both and walked to the water fountain on his right.

Felix's palms sweat, thinking about how the morning would go. He walked with Edith to the elevator. In a minute, his mind changed. He stared at the side of Edith's face. She wasn't like anyone else he's met. He put his hand on her shoulder, feeling the heat transfer to her. "Edith, we don't have to go back to the lobby. We can just stay on this floor until it's time."

Felix took Edith into a small lounge on the third floor, a place Edith hardly noticed while walking by. The door had fogged glass and there was no sign. Edith sat on the red armchair and looked at the galaxy themed walls. Shades of blue, purple, white, and black completed the aesthetic. There were black armchairs and a coffee table. By the door was a coffee bar.

Felix sat down across from Edith and gazed at her in awe.

"Was the room always on this floor?" she cracked a smile.

He slightly chuckled.

"It's been here for two years, but I guess workaholics never stopped by. I come here sometimes when I need a place to think."

"It seems like you've made this building your playground." Edith licked her lips. She leaned back against the armchair to make herself comfortable.

Felix brought his attention to her eyes as he folded his hands. An ice pack would be handy right now. He inhaled sharply and let his breath release slowly. *Edith, I'm in love with you. I love you. Just spill it out.*

"Edith," he cleared his throat. *She's not like the other women. Don't think about them, think about her.* "There's something I've been wanting to say to you and now's the only time to do it." Edith watched the light bounce off his eyes. Her heart was equally frantic. "I'm falling deeper in love with you." he gets up and kneels in front of her, not caring that he'd bruise his knee on the carpet or wrinkle his pants. "You must think I'm controlling or selfish. I promise that towards you, I won't be. I want to be more to you."

Edith parted her lips. He stopped the words, wanting to escape from her mouth. More. He wants to be more. "I've thought of my future several times before, but with you…" he trailed. "Everything seems so clear. I want to be your teammate, your lover. My soul yearns to entwine with yours."

Edith leaned down and Felix moved up to meet her eyes.

He brushed his hand on her cheek and held her chin, resting the other hand on her lap and inching closer for a kiss.

The doorknob jiggled and opened.

"Oh! I'm sorry," the older woman exclaimed. "I'm just here to grab myself coffee." she blushed, rushing to dispense brewed coffee into her mug. She kept her eyes on the machine.

Felix assisted Edith with getting up from her seat.

"I thought you said no one goes in here?" she whispered. He smiles and shrugged, turning Edith around.

"Let's just go,"

<h1 style="text-align:center">17</h1>

Felix entered the bedroom, leaving the door partly open. Edith hasn't moved from the bed since early morning to go to the bathroom. Felix looked at the silver watch on his wrist. The time read 11:42 A.M.

"Edith, come on." he says. "You've been in bed long enough." she still wouldn't look at him. Her dead stare at the floor worried him. "We've discussed this." he walked over to her side and sat on the edge of the bed, placing a hand on her hip. "You still work for me. It's my company,"

Finally, she looked up at him.

"I wanted to be on the floor with you. Now that bitch gets all her glory." she sat up and crossed her arms.

"Aren't you adorable?" he smiles. Felix kissed away her frown. "That bitch has Kyle to distract her. She won't lay a finger on me because she's not you,"

Felix pulled the duvet off Edith's lap and casually laid in bed next to her. Edith watched as he trailed his hand down her to her thigh. She pressed her lips together and allowed the tension to build. A groan escaped her lips while Felix slipped his hand into her panties.

"You're so tense," he whispered with a moan. "Relax a little." he pulled Edith's panties and shorts down to her ankles with one hand.

The tip of his middle finger rubbed against the hood of her clitoris and runs down her folds. Felix leans in, adjusting his position. That's better. He circled his middle finger on her clitoris to start the fun. Felix watched as Edith bit her lip down. He moved faster, teasing her slit.

He put his lips to her ear.

"I'm still the boss of you," his words vibrate into her ears. She could only respond with a whimper, holding her tongue. Felix continued to move his fingers in a circular motion. He parted his legs to give the bulge in his pants some room.

It's time.

Felix pulled Edith's shorts and panties down, then gently pushed his fingers in between the folds of her pussy. It pops out a dab of cum onto his fingers. "You should tell me when you're wet next time," he growled, pumping his fingers in and out of her.

Her body convulsed, feeling his speed exhaust her energy. Edith's heart wanted to leap out of her chest. Felix kissed Edith softly, pulled his fingers out, and watched the string of cum ooze out. He smiles before getting up and stepping out of the room.

Edith sighed, licking her dry lips.

Felix turned the sink on and lathered his hands with soap and water. Edith stood up from the bed and tip-toed to the bathroom. She stood behind him and kissed his shoulder. The two stared at themselves in the mirror.

"You know, your house is too small for the both of us," Edith mentioned. "You still want to be with me?" he quietly giggled.

"I do, but I want to move back to my place. I miss my closet and my bed."

"Your house, your rules?" he muffled the word rules through the toothbrush. Edith nodded. He took another minute brushing before spitting out the paste.

"I can boss you around for once."

Felix rinses his toothbrush.

"I'd like to see you try."

Edith took her own toothbrush, squirted the toothpaste, and stared into Felix's eyes as she brushed her own teeth.

"If you need me, I'll be in my office," he kissed her forehead. *If you need me.* These were the words Edith wanted to hear from him.

She laughed to herself, thinking about her office kink. She washed her face with cold water, rubbing the facial cleanser into her skin. *Thank God I don't have zits anymore.* Edith rinsed her skin before applying daily moisturizer.

A desperate sigh echoed down the hall.

"Are you okay?" Edith called out. She patted her face dry with a hand towel before exiting and shutting the bathroom door.

The light automatically shut off.

Edith walked to Felix's office, wondering what had stressed him out. She crept down the hallway to his office and pushed the door open. "What happened?" Edith put her hand on Felix's shoulder. She blinked at the screen. Within the message, someone wrote her name in bold letters. "I don't understand. What is this, Felix?" her temperature rose and she could hear her own heartbeat.

"I'll have to go to a meeting in two hours." he says, sliding a palm down his cheek. Felix pulled Edith around to his side. "But when I'm done, we're going out today, okay?" "Okay," Edith nearly lost her voice. Her stomach churned as if she had an unpleasant meal.

Felix returned to the parking lot after spending an hour at the meeting. He sighed, placing his hands on the steering wheel. Driving home, all he could think about was needing a break. As he pulled up in front of the house, Felix glanced at the door and pulled out his phone.

Get dressed and meet me outside.

Edith smiles to herself. She was already ahead of him, brushing her hair and staring into the mirror.

Where are we going?

Just get dressed. I'll be waiting. You have an hour, Edith.

I'll be ready in a flash, Mr. Radley.

She sent a flirtatious emoji and blushed. She's never sent him an emoji before.

She sighed at the sign of fog outside. Edith pulled out her gray wrap dress and laid out her white flats on the floor. She stripped her clothes off quickly and slipped the dress on, sighing at the perfect fit. She slid into her shoes and grabbed the rest of her things before running out the door.

Edith shut the door behind her. Felix leaned over the passenger seat and pushed the passenger door open for her. She sat next to him, admiring his gaze.

"What's the occasion? Did the meeting go well?" she closed the door and Felix locked the doors immediately. His shoulders stiffened, and he adjusted the gear shift. "Felix?"

"I can never win, can I?"

"What do you mean?"

Felix pulled away from the street and drove the car forward. "They gave me the options to hire more associates, layoff some employees, or branch out. I could purchase a vacant building and expand." His voice lowered. Edith could feel his heart sink like a ship.

She forced a smile.

"That sounds exciting. That's great news, Felix!"

As they approached the stoplight, Felix looked over at her with fear in his eyes. "I'm worried about you,"

"Me? Why?"

The fire in his eyes faded to smoke. Edith opened her purse and put the phone inside. She clutched onto her purse and stared at the driver. "You won't have to worry about me."

"I feel obligated to. I don't want them to lay you off." he kept his left hand on the wheel and grabbed Edith's with the other hand. "If they do, that would strip away my pride. I need to make sure you're okay,"

"I am okay. I'm still with you, Felix and no matter what happens, I'm here. You told me that too. You're here for me,"

"That's right." he smirked. "I'm always here for you," he glanced quickly and squeezed her hand. His eyes dimmed once more. When they paused at the stoplight again, Felix's thoughts couldn't stop. "Having you there, it just— you make my life a thousand times better, you know?"

Edith laid her hands on her lap.

Grinning at him hurt. "I trust that you and I can get through anything. I love you, Felix, and distance won't change how I feel about you."

She loves me. Felix adjusted himself and exhaled.

He gazed into her eyes. "I want us to get away for a bit. Let's do something fun during our holiday break," Felix breathed. "We can walk around town, or go to the beach. What do you think?"

"I'd love to go anywhere with you,"

Felix made a few more turns, entering the downtown area and into The Greenway.

He smiles, remembering the times his grandfather took him to the carousel and watched his uncle nearly fall off the horse he rode on. Edith might like the carousel. She rolled down her window and peeked her head out, gazing at the lights and signs. Her eyes lit up along with them.

"Do you like what you see?" Felix asked, making a turn. He looked over to his side, watching for a place to park.

"I don't think I've been in this part of town before." she replied. "So, is this a date, Mr. Radley?"

As Edith rolled the window back up, a little girl running down the sidewalk giggled and screamed. Her mother ran after her.

Felix chuckled. "Call it what you want, but yes, I'd say it's a date." Edith smiles at him and continued to stare at the people walking by. "Perfect," Felix muttered. He positioned the car in its space and turned the engine off. Edith exchanged a look, giving Felix the cue to lean in and kiss her on the cheek. "Let's go."

Edith held onto Felix's arm, shielding her face from the chilly breeze. Clutching onto him made her feel like they were an official couple. No one is going to stop them. No one around here knew who they were.

There were long lines for food as they walked by. Felix looked down at Edith. "Let me know if you want something to eat." His smile made the frost on her face melt.

The two headed toward the Ferris wheel. Edith led her eyes up. That's one big wheel.

"Wow, I haven't been here in ages." Felix mentioned, staring at all the lights.

Edith scrunched her nose. "I've never ridden the Ferris wheel."

"Do you want to go? I went on there a lot when I was a kid."

His Inner Child smiles.

She loosened her grip on her arm and walked straight. "Sure. Why not?"

Felix watched the line fill up and looked to the side. The line for chili fries was shorter. A little boy ran past Felix, nudging him on the arm. The child's dad shouted and apologized. Felix gestured. "It's no trouble."

The dad turned to his son and grabbed him by the shoulder, bowing his head. "I told you not to run like that."

As the line grew shorter, Felix noticed familiar long black curls and the ass of a woman that made his cock harden in response.

"Great," he murmured.

She looked back and the man waiting in line next to her did the same.

"Wait here for a second." The woman said, excusing herself. She turned around and smiled while approaching Felix and Edith. "Felix!" she squealed. "Hi!"

"Siobhan! Nice to see you again," Compared to the last time, Felix's tone dropped a pitch. Siobhan reached for a hug, but he held onto Edith's hand.

"So, um… I don't believe we've properly met." Siobhan turned her attention to Edith, eyeing up and down with a smile on her face. "I'm Siobhan."

Edith held her breath. *I know who you are.*

"Edith. It's nice to meet you," Edith couldn't bear to show her teeth. Felix tried to keep his feet steady.

"Are you two dating or something?" her eyes darted to Felix and Edith's interlocking fingers. She didn't know whether to smile or frown. Neither of them wanted to say.

Felix breathed through his nose. The line moved up some more and Siobhan's plus one waved for her to come over. "Well, it was great to see you guys," she waved.

"I wasn't expecting to see her here." Felix said, monitoring the line.

"Siobhan seems to like you. Were you two close?"

I remember her reaction toward you.

"We've hung out." he replied quickly. Edith stared long and hard, waiting for his mouth to say more. "I'll tell you more once we've gone on the ride."

They walked up to the window and paid for admission. The cashier smiles, handing Felix his receipt. "Enjoy," her eyes twinkle.

"I hope you're not afraid of heights," Felix whispered into Edith's ear.

She patted his arm, shoving away the idea of looking down once they get to the top of the wheel. They stepped up to the pod and an employee opened it for them. Edith stepped in first, sitting on the left side. Edith's heart pounded once the door closed

"You can't turn back now," Felix teased. He looked into her eyes, leaning forward and patted her hand. "You'll be fine."

After two minutes, the ride began. Moving clockwise, Edith felt the pressure against her back. She looked out the window, then at Felix.

"Felix,"

"Here we go," he grins.

She tapped into her thoughts.

"I wanted to talk about Siobhan. Was she your girlfriend or something?"

Felix lightly gritted his teeth and looked at her, concerned. *What?*

"No, Edith." he says. "Siobhan wasn't my girlfriend." *I didn't want her to be.*

"Then, who was she?" she dropped her eyes to her lap then looked at Felix's lips, wanting to avoid his eyes.

He's already told her. Siobhan was an intern—and then some. *Edith, please. Not now.* Felix sighed, blinking out the window.

"I mentored her…" he trailed. "And then… I hooked up with her."

Her eyes widened at his words.

The wheel moved higher. Both Felix and Edith felt the pressure against their chests. No one can use me, Mr. Radley. She inhaled and let her breath release slowly. "Edith, it's not what you think. I was stupid then. Believe me, I don't care about her anymore."

There's no point in arguing about this. We shouldn't. He shifted his eyes, observing hers.

"Did you have a girlfriend? Have you dated anyone?" Felix gulped. He wanted to watch the view of the area. He wanted to enjoy his time with Edith, but she held him hostage with her questions.

"I dated once back in high school, but it didn't work out after a year. I'm different now, Edith."

"I see," her breathing slightly halted.

"What about you? Have you dated? Have you.. fucked another man?"

She raised her eyebrows at his question.

It's always about sex with him.

"I had sex with someone when I was twenty-one, but we never dated. There was also a guy I met online and went on two dates with last year, but I don't think I've loved someone enough to commit."

"So, we have that in common." Felix held her hand as the ride descended. "Commitment differs for everyone. Edith, I can tell you anything you want to know. Please ask me questions." His superior tone made her shudder lightly. Their pod reached the top.

Before she could ask anything further, he cupped her face and wrapped his other arm around her, pulling her in for a kiss. The weight of the ride and her lips crashing into his made Felix descend to Earth. "You're my girlfriend, Edith." he breathed. "Nothing can keep us apart," To her, the kiss was now different.

She didn't feel a pulse between her thighs or an aching sensation in her abdomen. Both Edith's heart and mind were at ease. He finally felt like home.

18

Edith stared at the empty boxes in front of her. She folded her tops and pants then placed them into a medium-sized box. Felix lifted the other boxes and put them inside his car. He groaned at the soreness of his biceps. Edith closed the third box and carried it to her car. Felix stepped aside to speak with the movers.

"Thanks, Roger. I appreciate it." he says. The man walked away and entered the truck, saying something to the other mover.

"Are we ready to go?" Edith placed her hands on her hips.

They both stared at the now empty house.

"I'm going to miss my house."

"You'll still have your silk sheets," Edith pats his arm teasingly.

"I'll have my silk sheets and you," he wrapped his arm around her briefly. "Hopefully, the new owners will take good care of this place,"

"They will,"

The movers signaled to Felix. He and Edith entered their cars, preparing to take off. Felix used to live in a three-bedroom apartment with two roommates before purchasing his own home. His single-hood was ending. With Edith's car sandwiched in the middle, Felix couldn't help but stare at the back of her head. She met his eyes in the rear-view mirror and smiles at him.

Two hours seemed like half an hour without traffic. Edith exited her vehicle with the box resting on her arm. Felix made a few trips, walking in and out of the house with the movers and his things. There was enough space for Felix's beloved recliner and he installed the TV above Edith's fireplace.

An older man in his forties walked over, watching them all. "Edith! Hey," he smiles. Felix exhaled, thinking nothing of it. The man approached Edith with a grin. "What's all this? I barely noticed you were gone."

"Hey there, Max." she slightly blushed, checking to see if Felix saw.

Max was a recently divorced veteran who moved in across the street a year ago. He kept to himself but checked on Edith once in a while. Edith admired his burly, smooth frame, and square jaw.

"Would you like me to help?"

"Oh, you don't have to." she gestured.

"Please. I insist."

"Okay, there are a couple of boxes in the truck. I'm sure they'd appreciate the help."

"They?" he looked back. "I hired movers."

"Oh!" he exclaimed, laughing at himself. "I'll hop to it then."

Max didn't know that he'd be moving most of Felix's items inside. Near the doorway, Felix looked at Max, puzzled. Max greeted him with, "Hi, how's it going?" and set the box down. He walked back out, with Felix behind him.

"Edith, who's your friend?"

She blinked, confused, and gave Max an awkward smile. *Why do they always ask this?*

Felix walked past Max.

"I'm her boyfriend." he says, pulling out one of the larger boxes.

"Boyfriend? Well," Max looked down at the pavement and coughed dryly. "I'm quite happy for you, dear."

"There are a couple more boxes left to unpack. Then we can rest." Felix walked over and kissed Edith on the cheek.

Max looked away.

"It looks like you have things handled. I'll be going now, then, Edith." he turned without looking at her.

"Thanks, Max. I'll see you later!"

He raised his hand to wave and crossed the street without looking back. Felix watched him, scratching the back of his head.

"That was Max. He's one of my neighbors," Edith explained while grabbing a box.

"One of your crushes, you mean. I don't recall you saying you had a crush." his lips curved up a smile, but the tone was dull.

She ignored his remark and smiled back, lifting her eyebrows. *Jealous, much?*

"He's your neighbor now, too."

"Fantastic," Felix groaned.

Felix called the movers and he lifted the recliner with them into the living room. Roger stared at the decor as Edith's space was more traditional compared to the contemporary interiors movers would see today.

The couple spent the rest of their afternoon unpacking and putting things where they need to be. Felix sighed in relief because he had no stairs to jog. Edith peeked into the bedroom next to hers. She had been away from her house for too long that she'd forgotten about the plum colored walls.

"I hope you don't mind purple." she says to Felix, who laid out light gray cotton bedsheets on the mattress. Edith stared curiously, moving her lips.

"I don't just have silk sheets, you know." he breathed and grinned. "The wall color is elegant. Don't change it."

Her heart fluttered at the compliment.

"I take it you'll be sleeping here tonight."

Felix's reflexes activated, and he grabbed the pillow. "No way, I'll be sleeping with you. Take this to our bedroom," he tossed the pillow to Edith, and she nearly dropped it. It was harder than what she's used to.

Felix followed into the bedroom, noting the exhaustion on her face. After she placed his pillow on the left side of the bed, he spun her around and wrapped his arms around her waist. Edith couldn't protest against the sudden pecks on her lips. He breathed, letting out a low moan.

Oh, god. She closed her eyes, allowing this moment to happen. Felix laid Edith on her back, picturing pink rose petals scattered around her body. There was something about his silk sheets that activated his desire to make love to her.

Edith laid on her side, tucking an arm under her cheek. Felix brushed her hair aside. He turned and blinked at the shadows, looking for the lamp's power switch. She reached over and tapped on the lamp's metal base.

"That's fancy," Felix smirked.

The bright rings in his eyes entranced Edith.

Felix grabbed her by her waist, pressing Edith's bare chest against him. She inhaled his scent and brushed her lips against his. As they kissed, Felix ran his tongue over her lips and slipped it in her mouth. She moved, trying to position her petite frame well into him. The hood of her clit rubbed against his hardening shaft. Felix felt her heat through his boxers.

"Edith," he groaned, pushing her up to breathe. "We already fucked."

"Please. Let's do it again. I want to."

She wants to. I can't say no to that.

His cock pushed up, growing harder. It pressed against her clit, making her squeal. She cooed and moaned. *Should I stop?*

"Keep going," her voice faded.

Edith felt the soreness in her thighs from clenching them. She ran a hand down her skin. The increasing pleasure twisted inside her and ached for release.

There was a flash in Felix's eyes. He chuckled and lifted Edith off him.

"No…" she whimpered. "Don't stop," Felix kissed her softly, smirking lightly.

"Lie on your back," he kissed Edith again as she listened. He lifted her knees, resting Edith's ankles on his shoulders. He inhaled, bending down and holding onto her hips while pointing his nose toward her mound. Felix licked his lips and moaned. He licked his two fingers and probed Edith's center. She inhaled, knitting her eyebrows, impatiently waiting for his tongue. Felix rubbed his fingers to open her gates and pushed them inside.

"Ooh," she gasped.

He watched her reaction, pulling out his fingers, then led his tongue starting at the bottom of her slit and up.

He flicked his tongue and sucked at her sacred bud. Edith initially had her arms above her head but instinctively grabbed onto the sheets.

Felix flickered his eyes at her. Maybe I should have tied you. As he continued to lick, Felix's tongue found its way inside her forbidden cave. He couldn't stop himself now. Edith traced her fingers on the sheets, then grabbed onto Felix's hair without warning. He moaned along with Edith, sending sound waves through her opening.

He lapped her up, not wanting to stop, but knew it had to end. Felix continued the act by licking and pushing his fingers in and out of her. Edith thought her heart would give out. She moaned and screamed as delight shrouded her. Felix's cock wanted to take over, but he knew what he was doing. A couple more pumps forced Edith to erupt. Her hips shivered from the overpowering blow of ecstasy.

She clutched onto Felix's hair. Her palm burned and reddened, but he didn't care.

Felix took his delicate time, claiming his dessert and cleaning her up. His mind took him to the office. How dirty would it be for Edith to drip cum all over his desk? Once clean, Edith collapsed on the bed, exhausted and satisfied. Felix crawled next to her and laid with the blanket at their waist. He kissed her on the cheek.

The two laid in bed, and Edith woke up with sweat sticking on the side of her temples. She stretched her arm to turn the lamp off and Felix's phone rang on the coffee table.

"Wait here," he says, while slipping the covers off his lap.

Edith pulled the blanket up to her neck and snuggled her pillow. So, this is my life now. *Maybe I'll move up the ladder someday, but for now I'll enjoy my time with the greatest boss anyone could have.*

Felix's voice echoed while he said a few things and laughed. Edith's eyebrows knitted as she stared at the open door. He's alluring on and off the phone. She groaned and buried her face into the blanket. Her cheeks turned hot. Felix re-entered the room after a couple of minutes. The door squeaked.

"What's up?" she met his eyes.

"That was a manager." he says. Edith raised her eyebrows. "Not someone you know. But, I'm negotiating to purchase a building or at least rent a floor so I could begin anew. Brighton Tech deserves more recognition. Don't you think?"

"Sure, you can focus on other sectors and give more roles."

"I want my employees to work together, not against each other. The past weeks have shown me how some of these workers can be unruly… at least to each other. I desire discipline and respect. We can't have adult children talking smack about each other,"

Edith thought of how some people spoke about him and about her. She pressed her lips together and gulped. She pinched the bridge of her nose.

"I'm aware of that," Edith sat up with her hands on her lap. The blanket sank down, exposing her breasts. Felix sat next to her, nearly crushing her legs.

"I want to take you, us, away from that kind of stress."

His words sent waves of euphoria through her chest. No one cared about her as much as Felix did. He brushed the back of his hand on her cheek. She looked into his eyes, trying to keep her heart rate steady.

"Felix, why are you doing all this?"

He leaned in.

"Because no one else pushed me to do better or opened my eyes to see the truth about my company." he inched his face closer and kissed her softly. "Because you deserve better and that's how much I love you." Felix stared blankly and looked back at her.

She placed her hands on her belly. Felix turned to her. His lips quivered. "Edith, I feel like I'm spiraling out of control. Everyone is putting on fake smiles to keep either of us happy but our backs are always stabbed."

"I'm powerless. There's nothing I can do to change people because they won't."

"Then let us start by allowing me to help you,"

"How?"

"We can transfer to another building." he sat up, pressing his back against the headboard. "I'm serious. I won't go anywhere without you,"

19

With Thanksgiving break over, Edith and Felix were back to their professional lives. She sat in her office after lunch, pushing herself to catch up with approving proposals or throwing them in the trash. Edith finished writing before lunch started. She yawned and someone knocked on her door.

Albert was on the other side of the door.

"Hannah, Ryland, and I finished our blueprints, Miss. Walter almost finished his report." he handed Edith the papers and tucked his hands in his back pockets.

"Who's Ryland?" Edith's eyes scanned the paper, then looked up at Albert.

He raised his eyebrows.

"Ryland Klein? He's been here for a year now." A chuckle wanted to escape his throat.

"Oh right, Klein. I apologize, Albert. It's been busy. I'll go over your work and return feedback by the end of this shift."

"Sounds good, Ms. Rosu," he blinked away. "Excellent. You may go," she curved a smile, causing him to smile back before turning to the door. Seeing her team put in the effort improved Edith's day. She was no longer stressed about a silly job position. The workload mattered more now. Hustle and get work done, Edith. She sat back at her desk and flipped through the pile of proposals. One proposal caught her eye. She pulled the sheet of paper from in between the stack and examined it carefully. Bianca's words were still intact, but rewritten.

The following information is for our next project "Milo". Milo is an efficient cellphone-sized robot AI wired to ensure customer satisfaction. It will be there at every beck and call, see the customer as its rightful owner, and listen to their every command. This little robot will be there to fulfill their owner's needs. Commands include reading or sending text messages or emails, playing music, doing a quick web search, and more.

Edith rubbed her chin. It seems the team still considered reviving this concept from the dead. She curiously swiped her fingers across her keyboard, intending to contact Felix about business matters so they wouldn't have to interrupt personal time.

Good afternoon, Mr. Radley. I would like to discuss a project proposal.

Edith Rosu
Engineering Manager
Brighton Technologies

She walked over to her printer to scan and upload the proposal. It may not have been his role to give an opinion, but she didn't feel like turning to her team for input. After scanning, she emailed and waited for his response. She read through two more proposals before Felix replied.

Good afternoon, Ms. Rosu. I have read the proposal. I'll refer to the CIO once complete. Have you shown this to the project manager?

Felix Radley
Chief Executive Officer
Brighton Technologies

Edith stared at the response and rubbed her temples. Of course, the project manager would know. Laughing at herself, she typed back.

I am working on a few things at the moment. I'll be working through other proposals and will pick my top three, then I'll send them over to the project manager.

Sent. Do I even know what I'm doing? An image of Bianca smiling with a champagne glass in hand, laughing along with directors came to mind. Let it go, Edith. Just do your job. Her stomach churned at the thought. Everyone here has been easy on her. The only pressure on her shoulders came from the desire to pull through and lingering insecurities that crept their way into her consciousness.

Sounds like a plan.

Felix Radley
Chief Executive Officer
Brighton Technologies

Edith smiled at his reply.

Taking her phone, Edith exhaled and got up from her seat. Taking her water bottle, she walked out of the office and down the hallway to the newly added water dispenser. No one made eye-contact with Edith this time. *They must want these projects done as much as I do.* Nothing but mouse clicks and keyboard tapping echoed on half the floor.

Edith slipped her phone into her jacket pocket and stood in front of part of the wall. While this was a clever idea, it felt silly to stand in front of a wall to get some water. She placed her bottle in the compartment and tapped on the button to eject the liquid. It took a minute for the bottle to fill up.

"Radley's doing a fine job as CEO, don't you think?" A man's voice swayed by the elevators.

"You mean Felix?" A woman replied. Her voice was raspy and louder than his. The entire floor could hear her talk. "He's a fine young man, but I would have preferred Elijah as our superior. Whose idea was it to have a child run a business?"

More shitty gossip. Edith inhaled and kept her eyes on the water, filling up her bottle. She twisted the bottle lid on. Without a second thought, Edith stormed toward them.

"Excuse me, I couldn't help but hear you talking crap about our boss."

"It's true, Elijah would have been a better contender." The man cackles.

"Mr. Radley is a hard-working, caring man. None of us... you wouldn't have a job if he didn't know what he was doing."

"Who are you dear?" The woman rolled her eyes. The pin holding up her hair wanted to come off. She snickered, patting her hair. "Are you his secretary?"

"I am the Engineering Manager in this company. I'm not ashamed to stand up for someone who works hard, just as much as I do."

The woman laughed again and the man with her put a hand on her arm, whispering something Edith couldn't hear. They gave her a look. He stared regrettably and pressed for the elevator.

Edith huffed and lightly growled out of frustration. She nearly stomped her way back to the office. One engineer peeked up at her. "Are you alright, Ms. Rosu?" her soft voice calmed Edith by a smidge.

She blushed. "I'm okay, Olive. Thank you for your concern," she smirked weakly.

Olive nodded and flickered her eyes back to her computer screen. Edith entered her office and put a hand on her chest, closing her eyes. She set the water bottle down and sat back down on her chair. *Edith, breathe. Not everyone hates you and Felix.*

Branching out would be good for him. Felix called several contractors and business partners for his plan.

"Garrett, how are you?" he smiles with his teeth. He twirled his chair and rested his elbows on the desk. "Maya told you about my new purchase, correct?" he laughed. "That's right. I plan to fill up positions next year."

Felix pulled his desk drawer and laid the notepad. *Six months? I could build a house in less than three.*

Felix pulled his desk drawer and laid the notepad. Six months? I could build a house in less than three.

He breathed and nodded, scrolling on his computer for another contact. He moved the mouse and hovered over a well-trusted, familiar name. *Ricardo Bautista, perfect.*

Edith couldn't wait to talk to Felix. She didn't want to forget about what she had heard. She knocked on his office door and walked in, wanting to speak, but he held a finger up. The busy man was always on a phone call whenever she'd enter his space.

As usual, she sat in front of his desk. It was a pantsuit day. Winter is too cold for skirts. Edith's top, however, hugged her breasts, outlining the shape of her bra. Edith's lips pressed, and she tapped her foot, mimicking the ticking clock behind him.

He ended the call and put the phone down.

I'll have to call Mr. Bautista later.

"Is there anything I can help you with, Ms. Rosu?" he stood up and locked the door, not wanting to take risks today.

"I think you should go with your plan." she stared into his eyes. "You could open the door to new opportunities for people. I thought about college graduates. Having you as their employer would be highly impressive."

"If I may ask, where was your first job? You must've had a few before calling this company home." he twirled the pen in his hand. Edith watched as it rotated around his finger repeatedly. She sat back and crossed one leg over the other.

"Well, I took internships in college for computer science and I worked at smaller tech companies to gain experience. Then my coordinator referred me to Brighton."

"That's bright of you," his eyes lit up. Edith breathed out a laugh and bit her lip. She looked at his keyboard. He observed her gaze, sensing her heart drop. "Edith, look at me." She sighed, avoiding his gaze. He walked over to her and placed his fingers on her chin, lifting it for her eyes to look into his. *Stupid kink.* Each time he says this, her heart wanted him to take her. "Ms. Rosu," his tone was forming a question. "Did something happen today? You have something on your mind. What is it?"

"I heard people talking about you… by the elevators,"

She waved her arms frantically. Felix laughed and dropped his hand. He sat on the corner of the desk. "That's it? People always talk about me. They're just afraid of saying things in front of my face." he smiles, wanting her to do the same.

"Doesn't it bother you? I don't know about you, but I'm done hearing people talk crap about others in this building. None of this is healthy."

"Which is why I want to move you to the next building."

"I can't move on and have you suffer by hearing all these vile things."

"I assure you, I can handle it." he glanced at his watch. "If you don't want to raise further suspicions, I'd suggest you go back to your office." he held out a hand, helping her get up from the seat. "I'd kiss you right now if I could," he muttered.

Edith sighed again. "Very well. Thank you for speaking with me, Mr. Radley."

She turned to the door.

"One more thing, Edith, I don't want to hear anymore sighs coming from you," his demand made her knees weak. *Oh no.*

Edith turned and twisted the door handle.

"Understood."

Edith wandered back to her office and stared at the string of emails in her inbox. Most came from the engineering floor. Others came from directors. She swallowed and groaned. Edith previously couldn't sit here and endure wanting to be in a higher position. Now she wanted to tune out and focus on the matters at hand.

Bianca's name appeared in the group email. It would be against the work policy to send that message to the trash.

She powered through the last four proposals and sent out a group email of her own.

157

20

In two weeks, the couple had to prepare for another break. With winter quarter beginning, the company's demands increased as stores and shops around the world demanded for inventory. Felix appointed his staff to handle the shipments and marketing plans for December alone. He placed warnings to hold everyone accountable.

The sales in November shockingly dropped. They kept their top inventions in electronic stores and other distributors for at least three years before the next model. With a mind like Edith's, Felix outlined weekly plans with a singular aim: provide people with an affordable product that would benefit in the long-run.

As they know, not all electronics would last.

Felix and Edith sat on their new loveseat in the living room, warming themselves up in front of the fireplace. The smell of toasted wood and smoke filled the room.

"Why don't you get an electric fireplace?" he wrapped a strand of hair around his finger.

"I like my fireplace. It's homey."

Felix smiles. Now the citrus scent of her hair rid up his nose. He sat up straight and glanced at the bedroom door. "Wait here,"

He's always telling me to wait.

Felix returned to the living room with a small blue box in his hand.

That can't be what I think it is. "Felix," his name rolled out of her mouth unpleasantly.

He kneeled in front of her. The fire's orange glow beamed, creating a shadow on his face. "Edith, I know what I want to do in life. I had a lot of things handed to me growing up, and—"

"Felix, no." she choked.

"What?" His eyes widened and hands shivered. "Why not? I want you to marry me." he stayed kneeling and crawled to her lap, looking up at her with puppy eyes.

"It's just that..." she chuckled nervously. "We've only known each other for three months. It's too soon."

His hand opened like a claw, letting the box land on the floor. It rolled and laid flat. Felix took Edith's hands and stared into her eyes. "I want you to be happy with me."

"I am happy with you," she stroked his hair. "But marriage isn't something I want right now."

Right now; he thought. *I want to marry you someday.* He picked the ring box off the floor and held it in his hand. He looked at it momentarily. "Can you wear it as a promise ring?" he asked, joking. His heart squeezed. Edith laughed dryly as he stood up. "I want you around, Edith."

"You won't lose me,"

They returned to the bedroom, keeping the fireplace lit. Felix held the ring box until he could set it down on the dresser. They laid in bed and Felix was now the one sighing. He puffed air out of his cheeks and brushed his hand against Edith's face.

"I've thought about what you said before."

"About what?"

"About leaving if your promotion went down to shit." he says, weaving his fingers between hers.

She turned on her side, and Felix pressed his chest against her back. The bed became the safest place for him to be vulnerable with her. Edith led her eyes up at the ceiling. "Think about it, Edith." he continued. "I've been in this career for who knows how long and nothing has driven me to make changes. Nothing, until I met you,"

"Are you quitting? You have other options. You can't just jump ship now."

"I'm not giving up, but I'd dive into the water recklessly, knowing I had to save you," he laid back and stared at the ceiling.

"But if things gradually get worse, I can step down."

"What happened to the confident, charming, determined CEO that I know?"

"This CEO got lost,"

"Then he has to find himself again. However long it takes."

Felix's phone rings on the bedside table. He slides the phone off and puts it to his ear. He sat up with his back against the headboard. Clearing his throat, he switched to the strong CEO persona.

"Radley," he says, deepening his voice. Edith turned away on her side, wanting to laugh. "Is that so?" he asked. "That is astounding news! Okay, I'll shoot an email and make phone calls immediately." Felix bid his adieu and hung up. He put the phone back on the bedside table.

"Who was that?"

"I've made phone calls and contacted staff and contractors. Two of them would like to speak with me about purchasing their vacant building." he paused. "But I'd have to contact staff and teams who can prove our company is suitable. If all goes well, then a new adventure awaits." Light bounced on his dull, dark eyes.

"I knew you could do it!" Edith giggled. Felix pressed his lips against hers, deepening the kiss. She could feel his heart flutter.

Days rolled by and Edith's thoughts about Felix shifted. She sat in her office, taking notes for the people she spoke to. Waiting for Albert to report to her, Edith sat still, daydreaming about her journey. Felix was initially attracted to her, and he allured her in every way. His high sex-drive possessed him to take her as his own.

Although, he served as her protector; the hero she never dreamed of meeting in this lifetime. If it wasn't for him, they would've left me for dead. It was as if her car crash was orchestrated. She was meant to be rescued by Felix Radley himself. She shook the thought of him switching sides and using her. The man confessed his love. Who knows how many times?

Edith's mind wandered to Felix's smile, his laugh, and his smooth, toned skin, the way he carried her to safety and stared at her with those soft yet needy eyes.

Albert knocked, interrupting her fantasy.

Albert caught her expression through the office windows and looked forward, ignoring the fact that his boss was daydreaming. Edith gestured for him to come in. The others were clocking out at their usual times. Albert sat in the seat in front of her desk.

"You wanted to see me, Miss?" "Albert," she cleared her throat, folded her hands, and leaned forward. "I wanted to discuss a matter which you may know about." "Okay?" he looked around, glancing behind him to see his colleagues making their way to the elevator. Am I in trouble? He gulped.

Edith pulled Bianca's proposal out from the pile next to her and laid it out in front him. Albert relaxed his eyebrows and raised his eyebrows, recognizing the words on the page.

"What can you tell me about this proposal?" her hand stayed at the top of the sheet. "As I recall, the device mentioned in this proposal is an ancient concept; something that was originally scrapped."

"Miss Rosu, Bianca thought it would be a clever idea to reconstruct this idea. I know someone else came up with it, but other companies have something similar, so why not come up with something better to show the competitors how we can win against them?" His heart pounded with each word and he fastened his pace despite the surface of his tongue turning dry. Albert licked his lips and rubbed his sweaty palms on his newly ironed slacks.

So she slept with the Vice President and committed plagiarism. Bianca's worse than I thought. Edith pulled back her empowering gaze and softened her voice.

"Thank you for informing me about these things, Albert. It sounds like an excellent idea, but as you know, we are not looking to mimic other companies." she exhaled slowly. "We are here to create something innovative. I want something meaningful and eye-opening that won't bore even the most impassioned customers."

Edith placed the proposal on her copier and scanned it to keep. She handed the original piece to Albert.

"It was Bianca's idea,"

"I understand, but I had a hunch you two worked on this together. Since she is no longer working on this floor, I am counting on you to make the right decisions from now on. It might not be your title, but in my eyes, you are the lead researcher for this team. Is that clear?" Edith kept her eyes on Albert while clicking and dragging the file into a secure folder.

There's nothing she could do to hold Bianca accountable. She would run to the beloved VP or whine to other directors. Edith has plenty of hell's demons watching over her. Albert nodded and apologized for Bianca's actions. Edith didn't want to be hard on him, but as his friend, she wanted him to do better, to think about the damage Bianca could have caused by involving him.

Edith straightened the stack of sheets as Albert excused himself from her office. *I don't think Felix could be this tough on his peers.* He's too endearing. She could report this incident to the other managers, but what good would that do? No one would listen to her.

Edith's phone rang inside her desk drawer. She looked around before answering.

"Felix, what's up?" she smiles.

Edith giggled at his response.

From a distance, *Albert heard her say his name. Isn't Felix the owner of this company?* He slung the strap of his messenger bag over his shoulder and clicked to log out of his computer. He couldn't help but stare at Edith. She continued to smile, subconsciously wrapping hair around her finger. She turned her chair around and the conversation became inaudible.

A hand startled Albert, smacking him on the back. "See you next week, man." His colleague said.

"Sure, enjoy your weekend, Byron." he waved as Byron walked out. Albert watched Edith pack her purse and hang up the phone. He shifted his gaze and walked away from the cubicles, taking a detour so Edith wouldn't see him.

She glanced in time to see Albert leaving. *I don't think I should tell Felix about my conversation with Albert.*

Edith drove home with furrowed brows, giving herself a headache. Her conversation with Albert replayed in her head. *Felix may know about this, I think. But he doesn't need to know everything.* Edith has read and approved countless proposals from her team before. With a track record of being one of the best, it was unlike Albert to slip up. He was fortunate to leave without a warning. Bianca wouldn't vouch for him now.

She arrived home, feeling the emotional stress get to her physically. Edith opened the door and kicked her heels off, moaning. She left her heels by the entryway and looked ahead. There was a white mini Christmas tree sitting on the kitchen bar. Felix decorated it with white and blue ornaments and its lights blinked various colors.

Felix came out of the bathroom. He walked up to Edith and wrapped his arms around her, ignoring the patch of sweat on the back of her neck. "I'm so glad you're home." he pecked her cheek lightly.

Her eyes moved to his bare arms. She licked her lips at the sight of his dress shirt sleeves rolled up. "Is the Christmas tree new?"

"I found the tree in my box of trinkets just in time. I went to the store after my shift and thought the ornaments and lights would give a pleasant touch." He grinned at his artwork and placed his hands on his hips gratefully. "Do you like it?"

"I love it. It adds aesthetic to my house."

"Our house, you mean."

"Right, our house. I'm sorry. It's been a long day at work and the stress got to me."

He lead her to the loveseat. They both sat down and he propped his elbow, gazing into her eyes.

"I noticed. Was there a reason you asked me about a certain proposal?"

Her eyes widened. Edith rubbed the itch under her lip.

"I just thought I could get a second opinion, but it's fine. That kind of product is common, but I think I can work around it." I hate lying to him. Well, it's partially true. She licked the dry fading lipstick off her lips.

"From what I've seen statistically, virtual assistants make quite the impression on people. Even associates. But it doesn't hurt to create a Brighton Tech version." he says, allowing Edith to lean against his chest. The beating of his heart caused hers to relax.

"Okay, I just thought it was redundant." she cracked a smile.

"If someone wants to create some type of virtual assistant under our company's name, I say let them. Just ensure they follow company guidelines and stray from plagiarizing other company concepts." he chuckled. "We wouldn't want someone from Google coming after us with lawsuits."

Edith laughed nervously.

"If I were the owner of this company, that would be unacceptable." she remarks, forgetting the owner sat right next to her. Felix pulled her chin up, planting a kiss to settle Edith's nerves down.

20

In two weeks, the couple had to prepare for another break. With winter quarter beginning, the company's demands increased as stores and shops around the world demanded for inventory. Felix appointed his staff to handle the shipments and marketing plans for December alone. He placed warnings to hold everyone accountable.

The sales in November shockingly dropped. They kept their top inventions in electronic stores and other distributors for at least three years before the next model. With a mind like Edith's, Felix outlined weekly plans with a singular aim: provide people with an affordable product that would benefit in the long-run.

As they know, not all electronics would last.

Felix and Edith sat on their new loveseat in the living room, warming themselves up in front of the fireplace. The smell of toasted wood and smoke filled the room.

"Why don't you get an electric fireplace?" he wrapped a strand of hair around his finger.

"I like my fireplace. It's homey."

Felix smiles. Now the citrus scent of her hair rid up his nose. He sat up straight and glanced at the bedroom door. "Wait here,"

He's always telling me to wait.

Felix returned to the living room with a small blue box in his hand. That can't be what I think it is.

"Felix," his name rolled out of her mouth unpleasantly. He kneeled in front of her. The fire's orange glow beamed, creating a shadow on his face. "Edith, I know what I want to do in life. I had a lot of things handed to me growing up, and—"

"Felix, no." she choked.

"What?" His eyes widened and hands shivered. "Why not? I want you to marry me." he stayed kneeling and crawled to her lap, looking up at her with puppy eyes.

"It's just that…" she chuckled nervously. "We've only known each other for three months. It's too soon."

His hand opened like a claw, letting the box land on the floor. It rolled and laid flat. Felix took Edith's hands and stared into her eyes. "I want you to be happy with me."

"I am happy with you," she stroked his hair. "But marriage isn't something I want right now."

Right now; he thought. I want to marry you someday. He picked the ring box off the floor and held it in his hand. He looked at it momentarily. "Can you wear it as a promise ring?" he asked, joking. His heart squeezed. Edith laughed dryly as he stood up. "I want you around, Edith."

"You won't lose me,"

They returned to the bedroom, keeping the fireplace lit. Felix held the ring box until he could set it down on the dresser. They laid in bed and Felix was now the one sighing. He puffed air out of his cheeks and brushed his hand against Edith's face.

"I've thought about what you said before."

"About what?"

"About leaving if your promotion went down to shit." he says, weaving his fingers between hers.

She turned on her side, and Felix pressed his chest against her back. The bed became the safest place for him to be vulnerable with her. Edith led her eyes up at the ceiling. "Think about it, Edith." he continued. "I've been in this career for who knows how long and nothing has driven me to make changes. Nothing, until I met you,"

"Are you quitting? You have other options. You can't just jump ship now."

"I'm not giving up, but I'd dive into the water recklessly, knowing I had to save you," he laid back and stared at the ceiling. "But if things gradually get worse, I can step down."

"What happened to the confident, charming, determined CEO that I know?"

"This CEO got lost,"

"Then he has to find himself again. However long it takes."

Felix's phone rings on the bedside table. He slides the phone off and puts it to his ear. He sat up with his back against the headboard. Clearing his throat, he switched to the strong CEO persona.

"Radley," he says, deepening his voice. Edith turned away on her side, wanting to laugh. "Is that so?" he asked. "That is astounding news! Okay, I'll shoot an email and make phone calls immediately." Felix bid his adieu and hung up. He put the phone back on the bedside table.

"Who was that?"

"I've made phone calls and contacted staff and contractors. Two of them would like to speak with me about purchasing their vacant building." he paused. "But I'd have to contact staff and teams who can prove our company is suitable. If all goes well, then a new adventure awaits." Light bounced on his dull, dark eyes.

"I knew you could do it!" Edith giggled. Felix pressed his lips against hers, deepening the kiss. She could feel his heart flutter.

Days rolled by and Edith's thoughts about Felix shifted. She sat in her office, taking notes for the people she spoke to. Waiting for Albert to report to her, Edith sat still, daydreaming about her journey. Felix was initially attracted to her, and he allured her in every way. His high sex-drive possessed him to take her as his own.

Although, he served as her protector; the hero she never dreamed of meeting in this lifetime. If it wasn't for him, they would've left me for dead. It was as if her car crash was orchestrated. She was meant to be rescued by Felix Radley himself. She shook the thought of him switching sides and using her. The man confessed his love. Who knows how many times?

Edith's mind wandered to Felix's smile, his laugh, and his smooth, toned skin, the way he carried her to safety and stared at her with those soft yet needy eyes.

Albert knocked, interrupting her fantasy.

Albert caught her expression through the office windows and looked forward, ignoring the fact that his boss was daydreaming. Edith gestured for him to come in. The others were clocking out at their usual times. Albert sat in the seat in front of her desk.

"You wanted to see me, Miss?" "Albert," she cleared her throat, folded her hands, and leaned forward. "I wanted to discuss a matter which you may know about."

"Okay?" he looked around, glancing behind him to see his colleagues making their way to the elevator. Am I in trouble? He gulped.

Edith pulled Bianca's proposal out from the pile next to her and laid it out in front him. Albert relaxed his eyebrows and raised his eyebrows, recognizing the words on the page.

"What can you tell me about this proposal?" her hand stayed at the top of the sheet. "As I recall, the device mentioned in this proposal is an ancient concept; something that was originally scrapped."

"Miss Rosu, Bianca thought it would be a clever idea to reconstruct this idea. I know someone else came up with it, but other companies have something similar, so why not come up with something better to show the competitors how we can win against them?" His heart pounded with each word and he fastened his pace despite the surface of his tongue turning dry. Albert licked his lips and rubbed his sweaty palms on his newly ironed slacks.

So she slept with the Vice President and committed plagiarism. Bianca's worse than I thought. Edith pulled back her empowering gaze and softened her voice.

"Thank you for informing me about these things, Albert. It sounds like an excellent idea, but as you know, we are not looking to mimic other companies." she exhaled slowly. "We are here to create something innovative. I want something meaningful and eye-opening that won't bore even the most impassioned customers."

Edith placed the proposal on her copier and scanned it to keep. She handed the original piece to Albert.

"It was Bianca's idea,"

"I understand, but I had a hunch you two worked on this together. Since she is no longer working on this floor, I am counting on you to make the right decisions from now on. It might not be your title, but in my eyes, you are the lead researcher for this team. Is that clear?" Edith kept her eyes on Albert while clicking and dragging the file into a secure folder.

There's nothing she could do to hold Bianca accountable. She would run to the beloved VP or whine to other directors. Edith has plenty of hell's demons watching over her. Albert nodded and apologized for Bianca's actions. Edith didn't want to be hard on him, but as his friend, she wanted him to do better, to think about the damage Bianca could have caused by involving him.

Edith straightened the stack of sheets as Albert excused himself from her office. *I don't think Felix could be this tough on his peers. He's too endearing.* She could report this incident to the other managers, but what good would that do? No one would listen to her.

Edith's phone rang inside her desk drawer. She looked around before answering.

"Felix, what's up?" she smiles.

Edith giggled at his response.

From a distance, Albert heard her say his name. *Isn't Felix the owner of this company?* He slung the strap of his messenger bag over his shoulder and clicked to log out of his computer. He couldn't help but stare at Edith. She continued to smile, subconsciously wrapping hair around her finger. She turned her chair around and the conversation became inaudible.

A hand startled Albert, smacking him on the back. "See you next week, man." His colleague said.

"Sure, enjoy your weekend, Byron." he waved as Byron walked out. Albert watched Edith pack her purse and hang up the phone. He shifted his gaze and walked away from the cubicles, taking a detour so Edith wouldn't see him. She glanced in time to see Albert leaving. *I don't think I should tell Felix about my conversation with Albert.*

Edith drove home with furrowed brows, giving herself a headache. Her conversation with Albert replayed in her head. *Felix may know about this, I think. But he doesn't need to know everything.* Edith has read and approved countless proposals from her team before. With a track record of being one of the best, it was unlike Albert to slip up. He was fortunate to leave without a warning. Bianca wouldn't vouch for him now.

She arrived home, feeling the emotional stress get to her physically. Edith opened the door and kicked her heels off, moaning. She left her heels by the entryway and looked ahead. There was a white mini Christmas tree sitting on the kitchen bar. Felix decorated it with white and blue ornaments and its lights blinked various colors.

Felix came out of the bathroom. He walked up to Edith and wrapped his arms around her, ignoring the patch of sweat on the back of her neck. "I'm so glad you're home." he pecked her cheek lightly.

Her eyes moved to his bare arms. She licked her lips at the sight of his dress shirt sleeves rolled up. "Is the Christmas tree new?"

"I found the tree in my box of trinkets just in time. I went to the store after my shift and thought the ornaments and lights would give a pleasant touch." He grinned at his artwork and placed his hands on his hips gratefully. "Do you like it?"

"I love it. It adds aesthetic to my house."

"Our house, you mean."

"Right, our house. I'm sorry. It's been a long day at work and the stress got to me."

He lead her to the loveseat. They both sat down and he propped his elbow, gazing into her eyes.

"I noticed. Was there a reason you asked me about a certain proposal?"

Her eyes widened. Edith rubbed the itch under her lip.

"I just thought I could get a second opinion, but it's fine. That kind of product is common, but I think I can work around it." I hate lying to him. Well, it's partially true. She licked the dry fading lipstick off her lips.

"From what I've seen statistically, virtual assistants make quite the impression on people. Even associates. But it doesn't hurt to create a Brighton Tech version." he says, allowing Edith to lean against his chest. The beating of his heart caused hers to relax.

"Okay, I just thought it was redundant." she cracked a smile.

"If someone wants to create some type of virtual assistant under our company's name, I say let them. Just ensure they follow company guidelines and stray from plagiarizing other company concepts." he chuckled. "We wouldn't want someone from Google coming after us with lawsuits."

Edith laughed nervously.

"If I were the owner of this company, that would be unacceptable." she remarks, forgetting the owner sat right next to her. Felix pulled her chin up, planting a kiss to settle Edith's nerves down.

21

Snow blanketed the streets. Four cars had already skidded this week. Felix stared at his work calendar, scoffing at the demands required of him before the start of winter break. He sent emails, instructing his staff about their roles for the next week. It's Friday. Felix wanted to divert his attention to the woman who made him see that work shouldn't be the only thing on his mind.

Edith stepped out of the bathroom with a towel. She appreciated the gift of hot showers in the afternoon. Felix set plates down on the dining table. After boiling and seasoning the pasta, he prepared home-style spaghetti sauce and meatballs, following an online tutorial.

Edith patted her hair dry and entered the bedroom. She removed the second towel from her body and grabbed a set of flannel pajamas from her drawers. After getting dressed, she stepped out of the room just in time to see dinner prepared for her.

"That smells delicious." she inhales and smiles.

Felix pulled the chair out for her to sit.

"We've been going out to eat. I thought I'd cook something since it's literally a blizzard outside." he looked out the window behind him.

"I've always had to cook myself meals during the holidays. Or the neighbor would come over and join me," she giggles. Her hair fell down on her shoulders.

Felix hesitated sitting down. He looked at Edith's hair and walked into the bathroom for a hair scrunchie. "What are you doing with that?" she asked. Edith dropped the fork and watched him.

He stood behind her and pulled her hair back, wanting each strand to get off her shoulders. He pulled her hair up and pressed it neatly, wrapping the top into a bun. Felix pulled lightly at her hair so it wouldn't be too tight on her skull.

"I used to help my sister with her hair every morning for school,"

"That's thoughtful of you." she pinned her noodles and lifted the food up to her lips.

"I think about her and our parents from time to time." he sat down and stared at his own plate before diving the fork.

Edith scarfed down her food, trying to chew slower. She covered her lips as she chewed, feeling humiliated. "What are your thoughts on having a family of your own?" *Don't speak while chewing.*

Felix took the jug of water and poured into cups for the both of them.

"I'd like to have children one day." he says. Edith smiles, swallowing the last pieces in her mouth. "I don't mind having redheads running around," a smile curved on his lips.

A majority of his family members had black or brown hair, and the occasional green or blue-eyes. Edith's compact frame and radiant skin mesmerized Felix. That brain of hers combined with his would help produce the brightest, modest, and determined children who can take on the family name.

Edith coughed, feeling like she would cough out her lungs. She reached for her water and sipped just enough.

"What are you suggesting, Felix?"

"I want us to be official, Edith. Cross my heart and hope to die. I'm not looking to hook up with anyone else. That isn't me."

The bad boy has spoken. What am I doing? My future isn't going anywhere without him. Screw starting over.

Edith stood up from the table.

"Okay," she says, taking Felix's empty plate and glass. Her eyes didn't leave his.

"What?"

"Okay, I'll marry you." her lip quivers. "I want to be Mrs. Edith Genevieve Radley."

Felix's adrenaline forced his hand to grab the plates from her hands and set them back on the table. She wanted to protest, but he cupped her face and grazed his lips on hers. His heart jolts with relief.

For once, neither of them felt alone.

After washing the dishes, Felix checked his phone. There were three missed calls. He ran to the office, clutching onto the phone. He logged into the computer and scoured the inbox for important messages.

Bautista Inc. & Associates
Headline: Response to inquiry regarding building acquisition.

Good evening, Mr. Radley, I am Carl from Bautista Enterprises. — Mr. Bautista would like to discuss with you about purchasing one of our former locations. Please respond by noon tomorrow.

Carl Caputo
General Manager
Bautista Inc. & Associates

Felix tried to keep his hands steady as they shivered. He laughed in disbelief.

He looked at the monitor's clock; 8:08 P.M. Felix felt his heart do somersaults. *Ricardo wouldn't mind if I called him right now.* He closed the office door and stood with a hand on his hip. He stared out the window briefly.

"Felix, my boy!" Mr. Bautista exclaimed. "I presume you received the message my GM sent you,"

"Indeed, I have, Mr. Bautista." he sat in the office chair and grabbed a pen from the drawer. He placed the notepad in front of him.

"Now, don't be upset, but I have spoken to your grandfather about this plan of yours." he says. Felix's heart pounded. "We've made an agreement for him to contribute, and my associates have already created blueprints. They're only suggestions if you'd like to take them."

Felix rubbed his temples. "Does this mean the purchase went through?" Felix asked. He scooted the chair closer to the desk, nearly hitting the pit of his stomach.

"Son, your grandfather and I are great friends. You're doing well at your job and we are both happy for you." But? Felix pinched his eyebrows together. "So, he's agreed to pay half and you only need to pay the rest of the portion."

Half? That's unbelievable!

"Okay! That sounds like a great deal!" he grinned. The corners of his mouth grew sore.

"All I ask is that you negotiate with your staff and mine to get everything settled. My general manager will email you the details, but if everything goes according to plan, you should have a new building in the next three to six months. Think of it as my gift to you."

It would psych Edith to hear about this.

"I can't thank you enough, Mr. Bautista,"

"The pleasure is all mine, my boy. You have a good rest of your night and Felix," he paused. "Congratulations."

His words melted through Felix's heart. He had assumed his grandfather wanted no part of Brighton Tech or anything else Felix was in charge of. Felix's mind shifted to his uncle. *Leave him be.*

Felix sat back in the office chair with his hands behind his head. Edith knocked and entered.

He looked up at her.

"Did something happen?" she asked.

He swung the chair around to face Edith.

"On Monday, I'd have to contact everyone from managers to directors and contractors because you're looking at the owner of a new establishment!" he grinned widely, still ignoring the fact that his jaw was becoming sore from all the smiling.

"I knew you could do it!" Edith threw her arms around him.

"I have thirty-six hours to contact a list of folks to help get things going and then the process can take up to six months to complete." he placed a hand on his lap.

Edith knew to sit on his knee. She looked into his tired yet gleeful eyes.

"What kind of establishment would it be? Did you think of a name yet?"

"I thought about you and I want a place where you take the reins and just be yourself."

"Okay?"

Felix licked his lips and raised his eyebrows.

"How does Radley Enterprises sound? I want to focus on the social aspect of business. Perhaps, communications,"

"Communications?" Edith dropped her arms from his neck.

"I realize I was so hell-bent on the technology and robotics. I thought we should add more social and written skills to the business. Let's give people leverage."

"Oh! Then, maybe people with liberal arts degrees can apply and get a head-start with your company somehow."

Felix admired her lightbulb going off.

"I like the way you think, Ms. Rosu. They'll need a mentor, though." His lips curved upward.

She looked away, feeling a squeeze in her abdomen. Her cheeks warmed.

"I'm sure there are plenty of employees who'd want to move up to a leadership position."

"Sure. They need a leader like you."

Edith's cheeks flushed more.

"You'll fit wonderfully in that role, Edith. You're already a manager and most of your peers appreciate what you've done for them. Forget about what higher-up says. In the new department, I'll ensure you're the one calling the shots. You can be director when the time comes." he wrapped his arms around, hugging her tight. "I can make that happen." he smirked. She looked into his eyes and then at her arm. Edith pinched her right arm. Felix curved his eyebrows curiously. "What did you do that for?"

"I wanted to make sure this isn't a dream,"

Felix leaned in to kiss her shortly. His hand slithered onto her lap and squeezed her bare thigh. It sent an electric shock up toward her center.

"This is better than a dream, babe."

She couldn't keep her eyes off his hand now. He smirked, not wanting to pull it away.

The sudden news heightened both their senses. Felix positioned Edith's body, so she'd straddle him. Her weight comfortably sat on his groin. He lifted her blouse and reached around to the hooks of her bra. With one move, he unhooked the bra and tossed it onto the floor. *It's happening.* Her breasts bounced as Felix freed them. He cupped the right breast and licked his lips before squeezing her nipple and placing it in between his lips.

"Felix," she moaned.

Holding her breast in one hand, he reached his other hand up for her hair scrunchie. He tugged at it and watched her hair fall down her back. Felix stopped sucking onto her nipple and pulled Edith's blouse up and over her head. He tossed it onto the floor.

His arousal begged Felix to bury himself inside her. He pushed upward, making Edith moan. His erection hardened at the sound of her voice. Edith lifted herself up, allowing him to spring his cock out. Felix gazed at her as he tucked his thumbs into the sides of her clothes, pulling both her pencil skirt and thong down.

He steadily inserted the head of his cock and Edith lowered herself, making a shape with her lips as she gasped.

"Ride me, baby." he wanted to call her his minx as he does, but something has changed. The love for her was far more powerful than lust this time. "Ride me," he repeated.

Edith pushed herself up and pulled herself down, moving slowly to enjoy the moment. But even as the chair squeaked, Felix held her hips and pumped faster. She couldn't do anything but surrender and place her arms around his neck. She held on for dear life as he moved roughly.

Edith moaned into his ear, feeling herself gush onto his cock, wetting his lap and the leather.

"More," she moaned loudly.

He gripped onto her hips and moved her body repeatedly onto his cock. The friction between his member and her opening created heat matching the fire that burned inside him. The spurts of her cum splashed and squished. Its sound made Felix let out a moan with her. Intensity rose to the occasion, making him want to release inside her.

"Edith, fuck!" he gasped and sat still, letting his cum shoot up inside her. They rested on the chair and Felix cradled her in his arms.

22

Four Months Later

Edith sat and stared at the basket full of well wishes and birthday greetings. The newly hired Assistant Director Annie, walked around the floor, appointing a new employee to his spot. She knocked on the glass door, startling Edith.

"Come in!"

Annie entered with a smile, but her eyes glistened with concern. "How's everything, Ms. Rosu? How are you feeling?" she stood by the door in case anyone needed her.

Edith placed a hand on her protruding belly. At least someone cared to check on me. The little one inside her floated about, turning ever so slowly.

"Everything is swell, Ms. Ferndale,"

Annie sighed in awe. Being older and having two young boys of her own, Annie always had a soft spot for children, even in the workplace. "How far along are you?"

"Five months in May," "Oh, she'll be here in no time," she cooed.

"Or is it a he? Anyway, I'll leave you to your work," she laughed.

Edith chuckled and smiled as she shut the door. As her hands swelled up from the pregnancy, Edith felt she could only type ten words per minute.

She gazed at the violet, and white walls, remembering the bedroom in her house. She adjusted herself in the padded leather office chair. *Breathe.* Her eyes adjusted to her new environment. The other office was home. She felt like a guest in the new one.

Time flew. *I'm happy to be here, though.* Within the past months, Felix and his team worked tirelessly to hire members for Radley Enterprises. Nearly five hundred people agreed to transfer over and other positions filled up thereafter. When Brighton Inc. came to life, Felix was fresh out of school. In a couple of years, he'll hopefully be a well-respected millionaire by forty.

A majority of Felix's new associates were nearly thirty to forty years of age, except for Edith and a few others. The elderly had more than a few things to say about his fresh start. Felix wanted a drama-free workplace, and any gossiping would ensue warnings. With baby Radley on the way, as well as their first year together approaching, Edith and Felix planned to save up for a cozier, suitable home for three.

In his office, Felix sat, making phone calls and responding to emails. Once in a while, his General Manager would suggest hiring those who've disrespected him or Edith, for which he'd decline without reason.

He was proud to have Edith in charge of written communication. Her previous reports excelled but often ignored. His connection with Brighton Technologies would wane over time as he focused on the new business. His grandfather was more than pleased to have Felix carry on his own work.

After his shift, he texted Edith to see how she was doing. He understood that sitting for over two hours brought aches and pains to her lower back. She already took time with pacing around the office floor and stopping for bathroom breaks. Something regular employees would hardly do.

Edith typed back slowly, responding to his text.

I'd have to get used to my belly growing.

Felix chuckled at her response and put on a serious look. His lips wanted to twitch into a smile.

I'd have to get used to you being pregnant.

Let's get some groceries later for dinner. I'm sure you're hungry.

The hour ticked by slowly. He already clocked out, but no one would kick him out of his office. Felix examined his bookshelf, forgetting that he'd purchased Shakespearean classics and other ancient tales. The textbooks on the bottom of the shelf were essentially on technology for dummies and for how to lead a successful business. Compared to his other office, this one was smaller and more contemporary. His coffee machine went down a size too.

"If I read," he muttered, "I wouldn't leave this place on time,"

He browsed business articles on his laptop instead, watching the clock for time.

The room was cream-colored and instead of the vintage wooden desk, he would have an adjustable desk and a Mac laptop for work. Gray upholstered armchairs leaned against the wall by the door for visitors and on the left of his desk was a console table with drawers. There was a lamp on top.

Felix came across an article called Busy in Boston. A photo of his new building was under the headline and the author reported on Brighton Technologies, as well as Felix Radley himself. *I had no idea people monitored my businesses.* He didn't think of himself as an influencer, nor was he better than other tech CEOs.

"Look at you, you're killing it, Felix," he muttered to himself.

His grandfather was proud, but did his uncle even care? Felix hasn't said a word to that man since his second year as CEO of Brighton Technologies. It was best to keep his uncle out of Bautista to avoid trouble.

I'm all set to leave. Let's go.

His phone pinged.

I'll be there.

Edith stood in front of the elevator, waiting for him to arrive. Felix was only a floor above her. No one else was around to question them.

Seven months into their relationship, he was still paranoid about people seeing them together. Last week, Edith had told a coworker that she would occasionally take the bus to work. Uttering something about carpooling together to work would alert a bird about them as a couple.

Entering the store, Edith hooked her arm onto Felix, breathing carefully. Pinching and pulling inside her slowed her pace. Felix rubbed her back.

"You're doing just fine, Edith. We can slow down and take our time if you'd like."

"I don't want to spend more than an hour here. Do you know what ingredients to get?"

"What would you like to eat?" he asks, grabbing the shopping basket.

Edith tapped on her chin.

"Can I have salmon?" she raised her eyebrows, wondering if he'd like that too. Her body temperature lowered as they walked down the refrigerator aisle.

"That's perfect," he smiles. "I know how to whip up Miso Salmon."

Felix told Edith to grab ingredients as they explored the store. She hasn't visited a grocery store since moving into Felix's house. He would do all the shopping and cooking while she stayed home to work in the office. Her go-to meals for lunch and dinner were burgers and fries.

Felix watched her, not wanting for his fiancée to faint in the middle of the store.

As he walked behind Edith, women would smile and stare at him carrying the basket. He cleared his throat, keeping his distance closer to his partner. Do they not see the woman in front of me? He kept his eyes forward. The stares made his palms twitch.

Women at work didn't bother to flirt with Felix. Why would they? Out of impulse, Felix grabbed Edith's hand and twirled her around. He hooked his arm around her waist and pulled her in. "Felix, what—" he stopped her by crashing his lips into hers. With her heightened senses, a whiff of his cologne caused her to moan into his mouth. He slipped his tongue in before pulling away. "What was that?" Edith snapped when she didn't want to.

Her arousal faded. Edith scanned the aisle and heard a woman scoff. Another customer walked the opposite direction, opening a refrigerator and pretending to reach for an item. She tried her best not to look at Edith's vulture eyes.

Felix reached his arm around, resting it on her shoulder. "I needed that," he chuckled. Felix leaned in to whisper into Edith's ear. "Don't act like you didn't enjoy that, too. You're glowing,"

Edith went down the next aisle to her left for soft drinks. It tempted her to grab a bottle of iced tea or a can of Coca Cola. Felix would probably tell her to drink coconut water. As suspected, he followed her down to the drinks and grabbed two cans of coconut water.

"For you?" she raised her eyebrows.

"They're for you," he looked into the basket.

"Go easy on the soda."

The two walked toward the open checkout line, and the same employee from earlier stood behind the register. She grinned at Felix and smoothed out her hair. He pulled Edith to the self-checkout line instead.

"Let's not waste time. I'll be quick,"

Once they arrived home, Edith wobbled to the recliner and groaned. "My feet are killing me." she looked down. "... and my ankles." she pressed a button to raise the recliner's bottom half. She breathed as the seat moved back.

"Just rest while Chef Radley prepares tonight's meal." Felix says. He set the paper bag on the kitchen counter and pulled out the eggs, miso paste, salmon fillets, and sake. Felix put the eggs in the refrigerator and pulled out the bottle of soy sauce from the cupboard above him. He bent down to open another cupboard for the container of sugar. "Food will be ready in no time, ma'am." he calls out to Edith, who was half asleep.

Edith lazily grabbed the remote next to her and turned the TV on. Ironically, the cooking channel appeared. On the screen, three chefs lined up to get feedback from judges. Edith groaned and switched to a streaming app.

As the movie she chose played, Edith felt her limbs tap out. Her head tilted to the right. He won't mind if I nap right now.

Edith's mind took her to work. As her dream came into view, she was walking around the building, smiling and waving at every employee she passed by. A dark-haired man stood by the elevators. Felix turned around, gesturing her to come to him. Coworkers all stared at them as he embraced her and pressed the elevator to go up.

Felix kisses her hard, running his hands through her hair. The elevator doors open and he pins her against the wall as people stared. In the dream and in real life, Edith could feel the tingling sensation in her thighs rising to her pussy. She moaned in her sleep, watching her dream man kiss her passionately in the elevator.

The smell of salmon and oil filled the air. The pan sizzled, although Edith couldn't tell if it was in her mind or not. She sighed, muttering something to herself. Within minutes, Felix turned the exhaust and ceiling fans on. He plated the food and poured the drinks into clean glasses. Felix walked over and lightly tapped Edith on the shoulder.

"Edith, the food is ready," he says. "Baby, wake up,"
Edith groaned.

"I was having a wonderful dream,"
Felix smiles politely. "I bet you were. Come," he held out a hand. "It's time to eat."

Once seated, Edith couldn't stop herself. Staring at the plate, her mind and stomach were in sync. She stuck the fork in each piece and savored every bite. Edith licked her lips and sipped some of her coconut water.

"You're an amazing cook," Felix smiles, chewing his food. "I'm glad you think so," he stared blankly, with a thought shooting through his mind. "So, Edith?"
"Mhmm?"

"I know you mentioned college graduates working at the company, but how would you feel if my friend Siobhan worked there?" Edith gazed at her plate. Her lips parted. What kind of question is that? "You like her, don't you? I mean, she has interned at Brighton before and she's just as tenacious as you."

Her ears perked.

"Felix..." she swallowed. "Don't compare her to me. We are nothing alike,"

23

Just before Felix's birthday, he and Edith agreed to meet with Siobhan to talk about her role in the company and interview her. The month of May had always made him anxious. It's the third week and the first summer quarter of Radley Enterprises and the sixth year anniversary of Brighton Technologies. Edith entered the coffee shop two blocks away from work; Boston House of Grinds.

Siobhan was sitting at a table closest to the door. Two baristas worked tirelessly walking back and forth to the kitchen. Siobhan waved at Edith. She wore a silk rose gold top, black blazer and black suit pants. She sipped from her cup and tapped away on her iPhone.

"Hi, Siobhan,"

If I interview her with him, then she'd know we're working together. I barely know her. Bailing would just upset Felix. What do I do?

"Edith!" she looked up. "What are you doing here?"

What am I doing here? Felix should interview her alone. The little one inside her turned. "I'm just grabbing coffee," Edith lied. "Is there a drink you'd recommend? It's my first time here." she laughed nervously.

Siobhan turned ahead to look at the menu on the wall. "You should totally try the Capri Macchiato."

Edith's phone vibrated in her pocket.

I just left the office to grab something. Is Siobhan there?

Even though she didn't mind Siobhan, Edith couldn't help but roll her eyes.

She's here. Siobhan asked why I'm here. I didn't want her to detect anything. Does she know I work at the new place?

She'll find out. Keep her busy.

Anything for you; she sighed. She stood in line to order the macchiato. She looked back at Siobhan. I barely know her.

"Are you ready to order, ma'am?"

The cashier's dull brown eyes stared.

"I'll have an eight-ounce macchiato, please. Thank you." I don't want to be here either, Edith thought.

"Okay, your name, Miss? Will that be all?"

"My name is Edith. That's it," she pushed the nerves away with a forced smile. Lips pressed and the corners of her mouth curved like a doll.

The cashier informed her total, and the barista prepared the drink within three minutes. Edith sat at a table next to Siobhan. She leaned over, hanging on to her empty cup.

"Congratulations on your baby, Edith!" Siobhan gasped and exclaimed.

Edith looked down at her bump and blushed.

"Thank you, Siobhan," *Kill the small talk*, please. She took a long sip of the macchiato. The heat slaps her tongue. Shit. She smiles embarrassingly at herself and gulped down the hot liquid.

Siobhan watched Edith suffer, trying to hide her expression. "The coffee's good, isn't it?" Siobhan continued, leaning toward Edith's direction. "So Edith, I wanted to ask. How did you and Felix, or Mr. Radley excuse me, meet?"

Edith exhaled, letting the hot air escape.

"We met at Brighton. I was visiting a friend once, and bumped into him." She thought about how he rammed his cock inside her on the first day. What a friend he was.

"Oh, did you? That sounds romantic."

Edith inhaled and nodded, wrapping her hands around her coffee cup.

"So," it was Edith's turn. "How did you—" The barista and cashier went to the back for their lunch break.

"You know, when I met Felix, I was such a young intern. I was barely twenty-two. He was so nice to me," she giggled. "Sometimes, we'd hang out on days off," Siobhan's dazed eyes shot the feeling of disgust up Edith's throat. How long ago did he say the internship was?

"It seems like you two got along well," Edith lifted the cup up to her lips.

"We're pretty close," she says while reapplying pink gloss on her lips. "We went swimming together at a community pool months ago. It isn't far from here. Have you been there?" her eyes never left the compact mirror in her hand. Something's off. Edith felt the tightening in her chest. "I've seen those breathtaking abs,"

Months ago? Edith's mind played a scene again.

Felix and Siobhan were in the pool with his arms wrapped around her from behind. She turned and looked into his eyes. He held her close, her chest pressed against his. He kept her in his grasp, wanting to feel her erect nipples through the bikini top.

Any woman would throw themselves into the pool to have Felix save them. Felix opened the door with a smile on his face. He looked directly at Siobhan.

"Oh hey, Felix," Siobhan teased him with her eyes.

"Siobhan," he sat at the table with her. "Are you ready for the interview?" he observed her quivering lip curving into a mischievous smile. What's going on? Felix furrowed his brows. He looked over to see Edith's frozen expression, dying to let her tears fall.

"Edith and I were just talking," she kept the smile, resting her chin on her hand.

Edith turned her head slowly, looking at her, then at Felix. Hyperventilating, Edith went for the door. Felix's lips parted. "Edith!" he called. He stood up and darted his eyes at Siobhan as Edith walked away. "What did you say to her?" The fire in his eyes lit up.

Any stranger would run from his presence once that charming smile dropped, but Siobhan wasn't afraid.

"I just mentioned we had a little play-time back in the day. Surely, you remember." she stood up from her seat and swung the purse over her shoulder. She patted his arm. "Anyway, I actually have somewhere to be." she casually says. "She's a catch, Mr. Radley. Be careful with her."

Felix stared, pressing his lips together. This was a terrible idea. Both women left him speechless. The barista, who listened to the entire conversation, looked down at the counter, then turned away, scurrying into the back room.

24

Six Months Later

Felix canceled the interview with Siobhan, telling Derek from HR to discard her résumé. Derek believed she had the potential to work in one of their departments.

"I won't consider her as a candidate anymore, Derek. In the future, she is welcome to reapply, but for now, I will not interview her."

It's been six months since his last encounter with Siobhan. Her ignorance severed their ties. Felix ensured to give Edith and their newborn child all the attention in the world. Their month old son cooed in his bassinet. Edith was in the nursery with him, playing peek-a-boo. Felix logged back onto the computer and scrolled down the list of résumé files.

Most of the positions were filling up quickly. Felix wanted as many qualified employees as possible. A candidate caught his eye: forty-two-year-old Wanda Montgomery. She was a copywriter for twelve years, a writer for three years with two books published, and has recently resigned from an entry-level data entry job.

Felix dialed Derek's phone number again.

"Derek, it's me. Look into having someone contact Wanda Montgomery, and also..." he picked a name at random. "Contact Blake Johnson as well."

Felix appreciated how polite, attentive, and obedient the employees for Radley Enterprises were. He still couldn't figure out what went wrong with Brighton Technologies and how impolite they were being. A majority of workers respected Felix being their boss as time went on.

Felix rubbed his chin, moving his eyes down the pages, and viewing Blake's résumé.

Blake was a thirty-year-old undergraduate from UMass Boston with a degree in Business. Felix smiled at the choices he made. Derek agreed to set up appointments for the candidates' first interviews.

Felix regretted thinking about Siobhan and wanting her to work for him. Siobhan could have caused damage to him, the company, or Edith. Stay away from Edith. After the call, Felix walked into the kitchen and poured himself a glass of Pinot Noir; the best of its kind. The baby cooed at Edith as she let him squeeze her index finger. Felix peeked through the open door.

What was initially an extra room with Felix's stuff was now turned into the nursery, with lime green walls, new oak flooring, and decorations for a boy's room. The lime color was Felix's idea. A decal of The Amazing Spider-Man was staring Felix in the face.

"How are my son and fiancée?"

Felix stared into the baby's green eyes. They were slightly darker than the wall paint. He brushed his lips on Edith's cheek as she cradled the baby in her arms.

Three months ago, for their first anniversary together, Felix kept his word and proposed to Edith at a small park by his old house. He had always thought single-life was his fate, but Edith showed him that love was possible. In the middle of hiring new employees and learning to like Radley Enterprises, the couple was planning to move into a larger home closer to work.

Their life together as a power couple slowly unfolded. Felix was wealthy, but he wasn't the type of man to flex and flaunt all the money he had. He mirrored Edith, keeping things humble and comforting. One of the other things he changed was his fixation on using sex toys.

Prior to Edith giving birth to Grayson, Felix vowed to make love to Edith naturally except for one vibrator hidden in a box inside the closet. Every session was done by impulse, but met with passion. Edith enjoyed Felix's rough, slow, inviting thrusts. She loved his control of the vibrator. Although, the classic slow missionary style and him whispering dirty things in her ear won her over each time.

Felix picked the baby up from the bassinet and smiles at him. Grayson's delicate body felt like a feather resting in his dad's arms. Grayson cooed and smiles. He blinked slowly and turned his head to the side.

"Rock him a bit. I think he enjoys being in your arms," Edith placed her hand on Felix's back, adoring them.

Felix moved side to side, grinning with a twinkle in his eyes. Grayson breathed through his nostrils quietly, mumbling in his sleep. He moves his head and arms a little, making Felix stare in awe. The enlivened dad kept his child a little longer. Edith sat in the beige armchair placed in the room's corner. She thought about adding Grayson's name to the room in a photo frame, or perhaps plastered on the wall in decal letters.

Her mind now transitioned to thinking about Siobhan, a name that she swore she wouldn't utter or think about… until now. She looked up at Felix.

"Felix," she says lightly with air entering her lungs. "about Siobhan…" her breath halted. Felix's daze dropped. He swiftly moved the baby back into his bassinet. Grayson mumbled again before turning his head.

"I thought we wouldn't mention her anymore?" he says, standing next to the armchair.

"I was just thinking. You never dated her, did you? Did you date anyone else before me?"

"Edith," he breathed.

"Please tell me," she says. "You told me I could ask you questions. I can ask anything, right?"

"Right," he sighed. He motioned for Edith to stand up so he could sit. She positioned herself onto his lap, and Felix wrapped his arms around her waist. *I'm pretty sure this armchair could only hold one person.*

His lip quivered. "Siobhan and I never dated. She's too young for my taste," Felix chuckled. "I'm thirty-four." Edith didn't have to ask. Her skin crawled with the thought of Siobhan's age range. "What's your question? You only get to ask three."

Okay, genie.

"Did you date anyone at all? Did you have crushes?"
"Okay, that's two questions. Plenty of girls back in high school swooned over me all the time. As I got older, I didn't think anyone liked me." he groaned. "I'm pretty selective, Edith."

"Selective?"

"That's your third question, Miss." His lips straightened. "Look, I knew what I wanted and you captivated me, Edith. When I saw you, sure, it aroused me. My dick overruled my heart and mind. But over time, my heart opened up to you. You're all I can think about, all I've ever dreamed of."

Edith's eyes welled up with tears. Whether it was from curiosity or insecurity, she was relieved to know her place in Felix's life.

Felix shuffled the papers on his desk and answered phone calls a third time since the start of his shift. Today, Edith took a day off to watch their son. She was changing her hours to work in the afternoon, and Felix would take the morning shifts. His assistant Victoria transferred over from Brighton, as he refused to hire a new employee. He stepped out of the office to greet her and take back her up to the top floor.

As he walked around the lobby, the receptionists and people standing around smiled and waved at him. Some would step aside and watch him pass by. That's right, I'm the boss. Victoria sat in the lobby, reminding Felix of a shy new hire. She stood up and looked back to make sure she had left nothing.

"Mr. Radley, this building is to die for! Why didn't you think of repainting the walls at Brighton? Look at these marble floors!" she cackled.

A silent older man glanced over at her.

Her black heels reflected in the white and gray shine. Aiden and Riley, at reception, giggled at her excitement. They stared at her from head to toe, judging by the violet sheath dress. The gold bangles on her wrist clanked as she walked alongside the CEO.

"Victoria, this building has four floors as opposed to six like the other one."

"I'm assuming we'll be on the last floor." she giggled. "By the way, how's Edith doing?"

"She's doing great. I've transferred her over to work here, actually. I couldn't let go of that talent of hers."

"I bet you couldn't let her go, either."

"Pardon?" His eyes widened. I didn't think you'd remember her. He crossed his arms as she grinned. "Aren't you two partners?" she said with a tune.

Felix felt his face burn up. He pulled her to the side, grateful that no one else was around.

"What are you implying, Ms. Matthews?"

She breathed out a chuckle, holding her smile.

"Mr. Radley," she paused. "Felix… lighten up, will you? I've known you for four years. Don't pretend I don't know."

"Does anyone else?" he flickered his eyes at her shoes.

"Only I know, Felix. I'm thrilled someone has your heart. I'm happy for you." she placed her hands on her hips then moved her right to touch Felix's shoulder, smiling endearingly. "If she needs anything, let me know. I'm here for her too."

Felix smiles. His heart wanted to leap out and hug her. He held out his arms and reached around Victoria for an embrace. She exhaled, noticing her face was barely at his armpit. He released her and cleared his throat.

Being the only child in her family, Victoria treated Felix as if he were her younger brother. They were four years apart and matched by his grandfather after the first assistant threatened to embezzle money from the company. Victoria had vowed to take this job seriously. She had never liked the word secretary, so they kept "assistant" on her résumé.

Felix followed her to the top floor, and he pointed out the sections and mentioned names of new employees who would look up from their cubicles and smile. Felix and Victoria walked toward the back to the main offices. Each higher-up had their own office.

Previously, Victoria would have a desk right outside Felix's office. This time, she had her own room. "V. Matthews," she read. Victoria opened the door and gasped. "Felix! You didn't!" she covered her face, trying to hide her glee. She dropped her tote bag on a chair next to the door. "I love the wall color! And the desk!" her eyes lit up staring at the baby-blue colored walls.

She looked down at her feet, not wanting to ruin the gray marble floors with her heels. Her wooden desk was chocolate brown, and she had a white leather chair with an extra cushion. The computer on her desk was an iMac loaded with iMessage, note-taking and word-processing apps, and video calling apps for her convenience.

"Felix, you spoil me," she says, taking a seat at her desk. "Thank you,"

Felix tucked his hands into his front pockets.

"I'll leave you to your work," he smiles. "I know you were to start an hour ago, but I'll let it slide,"

He walked out of the room and closed the door behind him. Victoria looked around at the bamboo plant in the corner next to her and the mini bookshelf next to it.

Felix hadn't felt this elated in months. Classical music filled the office floor. It was his idea to install wall speakers on each floor to kill the silence. The management teams would meet on the floor to discuss proposals, then move to the new conference room on the second floor.

"Life is good," Felix looked around before entering his office.

25

Edith felt her life shift back to a neutral state. Her work responsibilities weren't too hectic, but all eyes were still on her. When she was Engineering Manager, it took her three weeks to become comfortable with the position.

As usual, the employees were initially afraid to speak to her. By the time it was her second year, they all joined and worked as a team. Being a leader came naturally to Edith as soon as she learned to treat her team as unique individuals with their own talents and skills. All employees earned their ranks by challenging themselves and working hard to move forward in the company.

Both parents worked hard to get to where they wanted to be. This was the determination and confidence Edith hoped to see in Grayson's future. She wanted to be an exceptional influence to current colleagues, future peers, and upcoming employees. She sat in the living room, remembering what Felix wanted from her. Edith delivered, showcasing her leadership to everyone.

At the office, she's the caring, daring figure who everyone looked up to, much like Felix. At home, she was a mother and a bride-to-be.

Edith turned the ceiling fan on and pulled out an old tower fan that was tucked away in her bedroom closet. She powered it on and peeked into Grayson's room. The baby had his arms raised, mumbling at the ceiling. They say that if a baby cooed and mumbled at nothing; it meant they were responding to a guardian angel.

Edith made her way to the kitchen to whip up dinner before her fiancé arrived home.

She pulled out the cast iron from the cupboard and prepared ingredients. Aside from watching Grayson, she spent all day watching cooking shows and researching recipes. She bravely drove to the store after Felix left for work, taking Grayson with her.

She immediately prepared the chicken breasts, marinade, onions, tomatoes, jalapeño, Mexican queso, fresh cilantro, and olive oil for her desired dish. Following a tutorial, Edith happily baked the chicken. As soon as it finished cooking, Grayson cried on cue.

"Just a second, honey." she tossed the towel over her shoulder and turned the exhaust fan on.

Grayson's face turned red. He wailed and waved his arms for his mother's affection. Edith ran into the room and picked him up.

"Shh, you're okay, Grayson. Mommy's here," she brought him to the open and picked up the milk bottle while swaying to keep him quiet.

Edith poured hot water into the coffee cup and placed the milk bottle in it to heat. The front door handle jiggled and Felix put his foot forward, struggling to get the key. Edith rushed over to hold the door.

"You're home," she says, kissing him on the cheek. Strands of her tousled hair fell from the ponytail. "Dinner is on the stove. Could you set the plates while I feed our son?"

"I'm glad to be home. What did you make?"

Edith lifted the bottle up to Grayson's lips. He put his hands on the bottle.

"I made baked queso chicken,"

"Now, who's the chef?" Felix walked over to the stove and inhales the aroma of queso and jalapeño. His stomach growled.

Felix carefully set the chicken breasts on each plate, not leaving a drop of sauce, and added scoops of rice as sides. He poured himself red wine and Edith received a full glass of water. Edith cradled Grayson for a while longer before putting him back in his room. She then sat at the table across from Felix. His eyes never left her as he took bites of the perfectly cooked chicken.

"We should start saving up for Grayson's college fund." he says with the fork nearly scraping against his teeth. "Isn't it too early to do that?" she asked, grabbing the salt shaker.

"He doesn't need to get a graduate degree like us. I just want him to have a proper education in the future. Besides, who knows where we'll be eighteen years from now?"

"Felix..." she looked at the wineglass, biting her lip at the increasing amount. She placed a hand on his. "All I'm saying is, the future is full of infinite possibilities and it's hard to predict our future. He needs to prepare for the worst."

"Felix, I can tell something's wrong. What happened?" she stared into his eyes with her brows curved. His eyes watered as he poured another glass and finished his meal halfway. He exhaled in defeat.

"My uncle and I hadn't spoken since last year, before your promotion flopped. Now, he found out about the business deal and partnership with Bautista. He's set to move out-of-state tomorrow."

"I don't understand,"

"My grandfather had always favored my dad. Let's just say my uncle was the problem child. Grandfather always pushed my uncle to try harder, to do better, but of course, uncle wanted another path." he sighed. "But if he didn't care about Brighton or anything about our assets, then why is he upset now?" he stared at the last drop of wine in his glass before making it slide down his throat.

"Grayson won't grow up to be like them. Felix, I didn't grow up wealthy but I know how important success is to you." she swallowed. "You helped me want more for myself and so I changed paths... because of you. You're a leader in your own right."

Felix looked down at his plate, trying to process her words.

"But you had it easy. My parents had always pushed me around until Mom died. My grandfather is only kind to me out of pity." "Being a breadwinner wasn't easy for me. Why do you think I moved across the country?" she put her fork down and sipped some water. Her chest tightened again and Edith thought it'd be her final breath.

She stood up from the table, and the chair screeched on the wood. They both glanced at the nursery door. Felix stood up as Edith walked toward the sink with her plate.

He grabbed her hand.

"Our past lives were different, Felix." she breathed. Spit caught her throat as tears slid down her cheek.

"But you and I are the same,"

It's been weeks since the Board of Directors have spoken to Felix about the decreasing stats of sales. His marketing team had recently laid out plans for Brighton Technologies. They added a couple of fresh faces to the IT department while HR discussed hiring more people for the engineering team. Based on Edith's record, Felix promoted Albert as Engineering Manager and Carl as Assistant Manager.

Felix groaned, rubbing his temples at the ever-growing demands of creating home electronics. He tapped his fingers on the desk.

"What else do they want us to make? A talking vacuum?" he murmured. Edith walked into the office with a cup of ginger lemon tea in her hand. She placed the cup next to Felix. As he lifted it up to his mouth, the tea's heat brushed against his cheeks.

"Cut down on the wine. Have some tea for once."

"If only tea could make my problems go away," he tittered. Felix let out a small moan while taking another sip of his drink.

Edith looked at the messages labeled as URGENT in Felix's inbox. *Good thing I don't have to deal with that anymore.*

"Babe, come here," he gestured.

"What if someone comes in?" she asks, folding her hands.

He smiles at the twinkle in her eyes, noticing her temperature darkening the blush on her cheeks.

"The walls are pretty soundproof and I'm officially in charge of you, so I order you to come here," Edith didn't appreciate his rough tone with her. "Please," he softened. Felix nearly lost his voice saying that word.

She smiles to herself and pressed her lips before casually making her way behind his desk. He turned his body to the side and pulled Edith onto his lap. Felix buried his face into her hair and put his lips to her right ear. "I miss having you on my lap. In a public place, I might add," he lets out a giggle.

Felix tightened his grip around her waist, nearly pressing too hard on her abdomen. He rocked the chair from side to side, awakening both their senses. Edith didn't want to refuse. She dropped her shoulders and leaned back against his chest. She rested her head back on his shoulder. Felix spread his legs so her ass was sitting comfortably on the chair. She glanced up at the ceiling and breathed before closing her eyes, allowing her body to relax.

Taking the lead, Felix extended his right arm and tugged on the bottom of her dress, exposing her new g-string. "Since no one else is here to order you around, I want you to come to work without panties, Ms. Rosu," he slightly moaned in her ear. "Are we clear?"

"Yes, Mr. Radley," *Touch me, already, Felix!* She sighed, awaiting his touch, and wondering if he needed a signal.

Felix pulled the bottom side drawer of his desk and took out a pair of scissors. He glided the scissors, snipping the g-string on both ends. Edith gasped at his actions as he ran his hand down her thigh causing her to shut her lips tight.

His fingers moved down with his middle, touching the hood of her clitoris. "Each time you wear panties to my building, I'll have the scissors ready."

She focused on where his hand was. Felix kissed the side of her neck, moaning quietly as his hand approached its destination. He rubbed her bud in a circular motion and moved his fingers against her slit.

"Ahh,"

She squirmed, and he patted her thigh.

"Who's in control?" he whispered. Felix pressed his other hand into her mouth. The heat from his palm against her lips acted as a drug to keep her dazed. He looked at the blank computer screen, watching seconds on the clock. Edith's lunch break was nonexistent.

Felix kissed Edith's cheek and pushed one finger through her opening. She moaned through his fingers.

"Oh, please," *Fuck, I'm going to burst.*

Another finger entered, and he pumped just enough for her secretion to leak. Soon, he inserted a third, growling low into her ear. Felix enjoyed feeling her widen inside at his accord. Tears spilled out of Edith's eyes as she came.

"You're a good girl for coming into my office, Ms. Rosu," he looked down. "Even better for cumming in my chair."

As he pumped harder, Edith wished he'd do more. *Damn it, Felix. How are you so good?* It's been months since they've been intimate. Felix's fingers soaked. He withdrew and stuck a finger into Edith's mouth. She sucked willingly, tasting her juices. Felix cleaned his other fingers, moaning at her taste.

He remembered gliding in and out of her at the office back home. Before wanting to do anything further, Felix pushed Edith forward gently. To make her stand up. Leaving the mess, he took her hand.

"Come, I have a private bathroom."

They walked over to the right side of the room and placed his hand on part of the wall. The camouflage handle for the bathroom door was difficult to see at the desk's angle. Felix pushed the door open and Edith stepped inside first. He closed the door as Edith looked around.

She wiped herself down with toilet paper and washed her hands at the sink. "When did you decide to build a private bathroom?"

"When I realized I didn't like sharing with others." Felix walked over to the desk with sanitizer wipes to clean the chair. "Well," he says, clearing his throat. "It's time for you to head back, Ms. Rosu," he smiles, tossing the wipes into the trash bin underneath the desk. "Thank you for meeting with me."

His wink weakened Edith in the knees.

"My pleasure, Mr. Radley,"

26

Fall season rolled by faster than summer did. While Grayson was at the daycare center, the couple gave themselves time to go shopping together. Felix was used to ordering things online and having his suits tailored by someone when it's convenient. Edith shopped for clothes seasonally.

Edith ran her hand through the suit jackets. Felix tailed behind her, bowing his head, and tucking his hands into his pockets as he always would.

Edith looked back at him.

"I noticed you don't wear suit jackets as often."

Felix smiles, then frowned a little.

"I'm a dress shirt kind of guy. The suit jackets make me feel old. I feel like a banker from the nineteen-fifties."

"Hmm, then you should lose the ties, too." she giggled.

The saleswoman across the room gazed at Felix and frowned upon seeing Edith touch the suits without pulling one out. She raced to the couple and licked her lips.

"Can I help you find anything, Miss?" The blonde was almost the same height as Felix.

"Um, no. We've got it covered. Th—" "

Actually," Felix stepped next to the woman, flashing a flirty smile.

Her sultry eyes mirrored Felix's. Edith crossed her arms, and glared, watching the two interact. *Calm down, he's all yours.* She dropped her hands and placed them behind her back.

"Could you help me find..." he continued, using his usual CEO charm. His brief smile and beaming eyes would do the trick. "The perfect slim-fit suit?"

The saleswoman glanced at the suit jackets, then at Edith for a quick second. "Well, sure, sir. I'll take you right on over to the other section. We have plenty of brands to choose from..." her voice faded.

Edith found a tall mirror and a seat in front of it. She let Felix converse and make his own selections. The tall blonde woman laughed at something he said to her.

"Ted Baker would do," he says.

They walked to the next clothing rack and Edith saw the woman pull out a navy blue suit. It looks all the same to me; Edith thought. She crossed one leg over the other.

The saleswoman giggled and placed her hand on Felix's arm. "Can I help you find anything else?"

Felix hung the suit over his opposite arm. "I think I'll take over from here. I don't want to keep the lady waiting,"

They both looked over at Edith's bored expression.

"Of course. I'll be on the other side of the store if you need me."

Felix walked back to Edith with a confused smile.

"I could've helped, you know." she says, pouting.

"You could've, but you're my fiancée, not my assistant. Let the woman do her job," he says. Felix pulled Edith close and kissed her right temple.

"So, you've got a suit jacket," she pointed. "She was highly convincing, and I've charmed her into giving me a discount."

They walked around the store for another twenty minutes, choosing a dress shirt and two pairs of Salvatore Ferragamo shoes for Felix.

Edith watched him pick items like they were cherries.

I hope this is a business purchase.

She watched as Felix spoke to another saleswoman, who politely helped him with the purchase. Edith felt invisible, but she didn't want to bring attention to herself.

Felix walked with his arm around Edith's shoulder. They made it outside to the parking lot.

"We'll take you shopping next week, okay?" he says.

Edith didn't want to purchase anything for herself after he'd spent almost two hours shopping at Nordstrom. She watched the side of his face, seeing how happy being with her made him feel. She looked down at her ring. How does the saying go? Happy wife, happy life? It overjoyed Edith to see Felix cheerful and with him around, she didn't care about the material things. She couldn't wait until the day they'd say 'I do'.

They drove back home, talking about how the saleswoman stared at Felix the entire time.

"Admit it, my charm helps," he laughed.

"Is that so?" Edith smiles along with him, but her face turned dull. *Just how many women do I have to compete with?*

Felix took Edith's hand and interlocked his fingers with hers. At the stoplight, he slowed down and kissed the back of her hand. The driver on his left looked over and gave a thumbs up. Felix glanced at him and smiled back.

"I'm yours, Edith. All yours," he smirked. "You know I can't live without you. I can't live without Grayson, either."

Edith gasped.

"Oh my god, Grayson," she exclaimed.

Felix had already turned the blinker on. He turned right and entered the parking lot to make a proper U-turn. "Recalculating," the GPS says. Edith punched in the address for Alphabet Rainbow Playhouse. It was an unusual name for a daycare, but they accepted to watch newborns for a reasonable price.

"Let's go get our son," Felix says, pressing his foot on the gas.

He slowed down as traffic turned heavy. Within thirty minutes, they arrived at the lilac-colored building that had multi-colored letters for the sign and a rainbow logo. It was quite colorful for Felix's taste, but he wanted the best service.

They walked into the daycare center and checked in with the administrator, who was the opposite of fun. She had gray curls, pale wrinkly skin, and a sapphire ring that looked like it came from those twenty-five cent jewelry dispensers. She glared at Edith, who shifted her eyes to Felix.

"Hmm," she says. "I see, well. Belinda will be here on Thursday. She'll answer questions you have and assist with your concerns." The woman blinked and rolled her ice-blue eyes. Once the call ended, she put on the best smile and moved her eyes from left to right at the couple.

"How can I help you folks?" Her pitch increased drastically. She smiles with her coffee-stained teeth.

"We're here to pick up our son. Grayson Radley."

"Okay, sign here," she handed a pink clipboard and blue pen.

Another woman entered the office.

The woman was in her early thirties and wore a light blue sundress and white flats.

"Mr. and Mrs. Radley, when you're ready, I can take you to the nursery." Mr. and Mrs.; Edith smiled at the title. Felix finished adding his signature and walked with the childcare worker. She bounced as she walked, and Felix moved his eyes away from her backside. Her hair reached down to her spine. "Here we are," she whispered. A low-volume lullaby filled the room.

Grayson blinked his eyes up at his mother. Edith looked back at him, hovering, trying to contain her glee. "Hi, Grayson," she says. Edith picked him up and rocked him in her arms. They bundled him up in the blanket she brought during the drop-off.

"Your bill will process this afternoon. You two have a great day." The worker says.

"I'm sorry. I never got your name."

Edith held Grayson close.

"My name is Gertrude," "Have a wonderful day, Gertrude. Thanks for watching Grayson,"

Felix says. Gertrude's pale cheeks flushed pink.

"It's my honor, Mr. Radley. Bye now," she says, closing the door behind them.

The two exit the building.

"Wait," Felix put a hand on Edith's shoulder and turned her around.

She tightened her hold around Grayson's body. Felix wrapped his arms around Edith and planted a gentle kiss, treasuring her existence.

As soon as they arrived home, Felix removed Grayson from his car seat and placed him in the bassinet. The baby whined and blinked himself back to sleep.

Felix left the nursery and entered the bedroom. Edith had laid out a fresh set of red silk sheets. Its vibrant color complimented a faint beige tone. He snuck behind her, leaving the door slightly open, kissed down her neck, and ran his hands down her side.

"What has gotten into you, mister?" her enticing tone caused him to spin her around.

"It's been a while since I had the chance to pleasure my office seductress."

He laid her gently on the bed and hovered on top of her.

"Seductress?" her giggles made him kiss her neck more.

"Edith, you know my love grows for you each day. So will my vocabulary."

He unbuckled his belt to get comfortable and tossed it on the floor. The metal clanked on the wood. Felix kissed her passionately, feeling her draw him in with her warm skin. He kissed and licked her lips, then pulled down Edith's lingerie shoulder straps, kissing down from her neck to her chest.

She closed her eyes, feeling tingles spark all over her. *What a rush.* Felix gazed up at her face, drooling lightly. He cupped her left breast and took her nipple into his mouth.

"Ahh," she responds. He squeezed her other breast and switched over.

Felix flicking his tongue on the nipple and switching repeatedly made Edith gasp and moan. He reluctantly dropped his pants and underwear on the floor. She bit down, craving another kiss. Felix pulled her legs off the edge of the bed, meeting his hips with hers.

He teased her slit with the head of his cock, moving up and down. Her dilating pupils wanted more than just silly foreplay.

Felix pushed the head of his cock inside her, groaning at the feel of her pussy closing on it. He moved carefully, not wanting to break her. He kissed her cheek and breathed into her ear. She cooed and whimpered in response. "This is what I wanted the other day," he whispered, pumping slowly.

"This is so much better," she moaned.

His thrusts became harder.

"Noted,"

Edith's sides grew sore. He lifted her right leg, stretching it toward the ceiling. The way she moaned and called out his name sounded like music to his ears. Felix held onto her legs and kissed her calves. He wanted his fiancée to cum for him. Her cries filled the room, and she wet the fresh sheets.

Grayson's own cries vibrated through the wall. Felix pulled out as he and Edith laughed nervously at the timing. He assisted her up, and she tugged at her lingerie.

"I've got him this time," he says. "I want you to lie down. Get some rest."

Felix pulled his underwear and pants back up. He kissed her forehead before leaving. Edith smiles, feeling her own pulse. She laid in bed and tucked herself in.

Her fiancé was in the other room, making their baby giggle. In the most childish tone, he says, "Hi, buddy! Who's hungry?"

For the future of their relationship, this was progress.

Edith stretched her arms and back, yawning. She went into the office and logged into the computer. Felix was in the living room mumbling nonsense to the baby. Edith looked back, wondering if she should hold Grayson, but didn't want to ruin Felix's mood. She browsed the electronic store website for a new computer, a laptop of her own.

Felix had sold his desktop computer and kept his laptop for family use. *It's a hassle bringing this thing in and out of the office*, Edith groaned.

She scrolled until she found suitable specifications. Felix knocked on the door even though it was wide open.

"What are you up to?"

Edith glanced back at him. She smiles and turned to the screen. "I want to buy a laptop. Yours is great, but I need something for my use."

The blue light caused her to blink and squint at the screen.

"Are you hiding something, Ms. Rosu?" he chuckled. Grayson babbled at his dad. "Wouldn't it be convenient if Brighton Tech built their own computers? I could have the engineers make blueprints and you'd be the first to try it out." he looked down at Grayson as if the baby would respond.

"That sounds like a fun concept, but it would take years to implement. I need a computer now," her tone lowered to a near growl.

Felix placed his hand on her shoulder.

"Hey, don't sweat it, baby. It was only a suggestion. I can look for the perfect computer and buy it for you." She looked up at her fiancé. Grayson flailed his arms. On cue, Felix handed him over to her and she moved to the armchair. "You remember Victoria, right?" Felix asked, straightening his back and looking down at his shoes.

"Of course I do," Edith's eyes scanned up at him. "Well, you might get the chance to meet her. She settled into the new office next to mine and I might have mentioned that you worked for Radley Enterprises now." His tone was giving her clues.

She looked at Grayson, then squinted her eyes at Felix, who now sat in the office chair with his palms resting on his lap. "That's great. I'd love to meet her. Did you tell her anything else?"

"She knows you and I are together." he spilled. "That's not a problem, is it?"

"How do you know she won't gossip about us?" she breathed.

"I trust her, Edith. Victoria is like family to me. She won't tell a soul," he glanced at Grayson. "I'd like you to meet her in person. You two might get along well."

Edith felt her heart simmer down. She listened to Grayson breathe as he fell asleep again.

I should feed him soon.

"When can I meet her?" her lips twitched into a smile.

"We're busy this week. I'll let her know ahead of time to plan something so we can all hang out next week." he stood up and leaned down for a peck.

"I look forward to meeting her,"

The new week swept by faster than they realized.

Victoria threw her arms around Edith. She was taller than expected. Edith looked down at Victoria's two-inch Louboutin heels. *How much does Felix pay you to afford those?* Edith cursed at her distaste for expensive things. Compared to Edith, Victoria was graceful, yet bubbly and sweet.

The cold autumn breeze pushed her slightly toward Edith, and she smiles warmly, wanting to welcome her.

"I can't believe it's you, Edith!" she hooked her arm around Edith, giving a light squeeze.

Edith was uncomfortable with Victoria's fairly enormous chest pressed against hers. Felix squinted at the sunlight, smirking at the two but kept his posture.

"We should continue walking," he gestures.

He pushed the stroller, and Grayson squealed at the sight of his dad's face. Around them were duck statues. Swan Boats passed them by slowly. They walked a little further and Victoria gasped in awe.

"You're quiet in the office," Felix muttered. Edith nudged his side. "Ow!"

"You picked a brilliant spot for us, Victoria," she says.

Victoria slowed down for the couple to keep up with her. She walked to Edith's right side.

"So Edith, how long did you work for Brighton? It's a shame we hadn't met earlier."

"I hit my sixth-year mark shortly before moving on to Radley Enterprises."

"She was looking forward to becoming the Director of Engineering before they handed it to Bianca." Felix added.

"Oh, okay." she teases. "So you knew her before the acquisition." Victoria smirked at Felix. He let out a nervous chuckle. "I'm surprised you two have a child already, but it's not a bad thing." she grinned at the baby. Grayson matched her smile. "He's adorable."

As they strolled, children ran by and groups of parents followed after.

"We'd be like them someday," Edith mentioned. She stopped her tracks. Felix and Victoria both knitted their brows. "We can get married here,"

"What?" Felix chimed.

"Let's get married here, Felix. We don't need a large wedding and Victoria knows our situation, so it'll be perfect."

"That is perfect! We can plan everything and I can help you choose a dress. It'll be fun!" Victoria couldn't catch her breath.

27

From the first day they met to conversations they've had, and office drama endured, Felix and Edith knew they were made for each other. A lot can change in a year, but they surpassed the ebbs and flows. Before the wedding date, Felix called Gertrude ahead of time so she could watch Grayson at the daycare.

Edith held the flowers in her hand and stared at Felix from the back. He looked into the water, possibly reciting the vows in his mind.

Victoria stepped behind Edith with the clipped veil in her hand. She secured the hairpiece on the knot. Edith's natural auburn waves flowed below her shoulders. She didn't want the prim office look for her special day. "You look like a queen, Edith." Victoria giggled.

Edith wore a white backless lace wedding dress with a short train. The dress hugged every curve and inch of her body.

Victoria looked just as striking with her frost blue tones for makeup and a fitted charcoal gray maxi dress. She swapped the Louboutin heels for modest cream ballet flats.

Felix peeked over his shoulder, feeling as nervous as Edith did. He smirked at the glimpse of her utter beauty.

They all waited for the officiant to arrive and the ceremony began. While Victoria had only known Edith for a minute, she could feel love radiating from the couple.

Wherever life takes us, you and I will cherish each other for as long as we shall live.

The words fell out of Felix's mouth without a sweat, but his hands trembled. Edith wiped the tears from her eyes, sniffling. She felt his heart call out to her.

My love, forever and always.

Felix cupped her face and kissed her with great emotion. He wept with joy, along with the woman he could now call his wife. Her eyes begged him to sweep her away immediately.

After the ceremony, they were off to a dinner reservation that Victoria paid for. This was the least she could do for the man who made the workplace her home. On the way back to the rental car, Felix couldn't help but gawk at Edith from behind. Her hips swayed as she walked, slower than when she would hustle around the office floor. He sucked in his teeth and tapped his foot while the driver opened the backseat door for them.

Edith slid into the seat, feeling like a giddy teenager with her prom date. *Never in a million years would I think I'd be riding a limo.* Felix followed her in. Victoria drove her own vehicle, tailing behind them.

Edith looked at her husband. He kissed her once more. "I just remembered. Isn't this the suit you bought months ago?"

"Are you surprised that it still fits?" he smiles. She imagined his abs underneath. "I didn't want to waste it on some boring conference meeting,"

"It looks good on you," she bit her lip.

He leaned, touching her shoulder. "You look divine in this dress, but I can't wait to take it off," he whispered.

Edith swallowed, feeling the heat rise from her neck to her face. The driver glanced into the rearview mirror, prompting Felix to sit up straight.

"We'll be arriving at the restaurant in just a few minutes, sir."

"No rush," Felix chuckled.

Being the powerful man that he was, Felix could request a secure, private dine-in. Since Victoria was in charge of the meal portion, he had only requested a private section of the restaurant.

For a table of four, they could order the best French delicacies and the wine was courtesy of the restaurant owner. Today was the only time Edith felt self-conscious of her figure. She took a small bite of her steak and barely touched the champagne.

"Are you feeling okay, Edith?" Victoria asked.

She asked the server to fill up a glass of water and to leave the pitcher.

"It's a little hot in here," Edith says, taking the napkin and patting down her neck.

"You don't have to finish the drink. Have some water,"

Edith took a breath and, within minutes, she ate her steak halfway. *Why am I like this?* Her stomach inflated from being filled up with food. The stretch made her lips curve downward.

"Excuse me," she said.

She rushed to the private bathroom and locked the door. Edith splashed cold water on her arms and face then wiped away the blush. *It'll be okay, Edith. You'll be out of here soon.*

A knock on the door made her gasp and back away from the sink.

"Edith, are you okay in there?" Felix's voice echoed through the door.

"I'm alright. I'll be out in a minute," she exhaled.

"Can you please open the door?" She unlocked and turned the handle. Felix pushed himself into the bathroom, not realizing how small it was. "Hey, are you okay? Do you want to go?" he put his hands on Edith's waist, wanting to steady her.

"I just had jitters." she breathed. Edith turned to the sink and splashed water on her wrists again.

"Baby, look at me." he gazed into her eyes. "Did I make you nervous?"

Her eyes fell to his lips. She jumped up and wrapped her arms around his neck, planting her lips on his. Felix stumbles with his back against the door. He pressed the lock and led his hand down her back. "Edith," he groaned.

Edith kissed him harder than he'd kiss her, awakening the bulge in his pants. He lifted her up onto the sink and held her still. She felt drops of water press against the dress. Edith closed her eyes, pulling him into her. Felix looked into the mirror briefly, seeing the lust in his eyes. She continued to kiss and peck on his lips. "Edith," he repeated.

She dropped her arms. The booze spiraled in her brain. "I'm sorry," she looked at the palms of her hands.

"Victoria is here," he lowered his voice.

"I can take you to a hotel… after dinner."

"I thought we were going home after?" Felix shook his head.

"I know what you want and I want it too,"

The newlyweds laid in their hotel bed. Felix unbuttoned his dress shirt and stripped it off, placing it on the chair with his tie and dress pants. He tucked his Ferragamo shoes next to Edith's heels under the chair. The laced fabric embedded on her skin as she rolled onto her back. Felix pushed her hair aside and kissed her gently while caressing her cheek.

The fading eyeshadow and eyebrow powder revealed Edith's natural beauty. Felix kissed away the paint off her lips. She lifted her hips as he pulled her dress up slowly and slid off her thong. At the foot of the bed, the bewitched husband took a mental picture of his wife. He traced his fingers up to her thigh, pulling the dress with his other hand. The room was cold and dim, causing Edith to unwind.

Felix kissed the inner parts of her thighs. His stubble tickled her and sent waves of electricity. Finding her center, Felix used his left hand to tease Edith's slit and dove in with his tongue. He sensually licked her labia and moved around the slit, moistening her up. "Felix," she breathed.

He plunged one finger into her gently, working in and out for her pleasure to build, then added the next finger. Edith bucked her hips, holding onto as many pillows as she could. His tongue reached for her clitoris, driving her mad. Felix licked and flicked his tongue while his fingers did their job.

Edith was losing her grip, moaning in ecstasy, feeling waves of emotions ride in her veins. Felix saw the agony in her eyes.

He straightened her legs gently on the bed and hovered over her. Edith pulled him closer to her, wanting skin to skin.

"I don't want to break you," he breathes.

"Then go easy on me,"

Felix lowers himself onto her, carefully probing her inside. Edith gasped at the length as if it's their first time. She widened her legs to give him room as he entered her completely. Edith cupped his face, outlining his jaw with her fingers.

The cotton sheets rubbed against her skin with each movement. Each time Edith whined and moaned, Felix brushed his lips against hers and swallowed each sound through a gentle kiss. His hard yet slow thrusts tempted him to roughen his pecks.

"I made love to my boss," she giggled.

"You made love to your husband,"

Felix hungrily kissed Edith, giving her more chances to gasp and moan. He felt his cock pulse. There was horror flashing in her eyes. *He's going to stain the dress.* Felix touched her flushed cheek and clashed his lips with hers, allowing the moment to unfold. Felix giggled at the rush, fading his wife's worries away. Edith slid off the bed carefully and stripped off her dress. She hung the wedding dress delicately. Both naked, they laid in bed, ending the night drenched and satisfied.

Edith loved feeling Felix press against her as they slept, spooning. He kissed her cheek, and she blinked groggily. He smiles with his eyes.

"Good morning, Mrs. Radley,"

"Good morning, Mr. Radley," she smiles, turning to kiss his lips. She inhaled his scent, not wanting to stop.

Felix kissed back briefly before pulling the comforter off.

"We'll be having breakfast with Victoria and then after, I'll be taking you somewhere."

Felix smiles, pulling the suitcases from beside the closet.

"This wasn't the honeymoon?"

He shook his head and laughed. Edith helped with pulling the zippers open. He handed Edith a towel, and she bent down to grab some fresh clothes.

At the restaurant, Edith watched Victoria's hands move as she spoke, leaning forward to hear what Victoria had to say.

"I remember the moment his grandfather spoke to me," she says. "Felix was hiring and firing assistants left and right because they didn't exceed expectations."

Felix pressed his lips against the ice-cold glass and took his time with the sip.

"My grandfather insisted on partnering with the best. Someone who wouldn't run out on me," he swallowed. "I still remember being burned by these cowards,"

Edith placed her hand over his and squeezed. They looked into each other's eyes before Victoria continued speaking.

Victoria mentioned meeting Felix's grandfather last minute at the opening for Brighton's gaming console convention. This was while Edith was midway through her second year working for the company. She remembered standing in the crowd, trying to watch the presentation.

The memory flashed before her eyes.

Victoria stood in front of the stage with the executives. Felix and his grandfather stood on the stage, front and center. "We will release the BTech 1000 this summer. The console will price at three-hundred dollars. We will sell accessories separately." Hundreds of guests clapped and cheered at the announcement. Edith was among the back crowd, in awe of the event. She tried standing on her toes to see clearly.

It's surreal to think she was sitting with the CEO now, as his wife. Those days are gone.

Victoria took a sip of water.

"Felix was such a young man when I met him. The Radleys are nice people, Edith."
Felix chuckled nervously.

28

Edith exited the building and walked across the street to Swan Café & Bakery. Felix stayed late to mentor new employees, who waited two weeks for a response from him. Edith walked into the coffee shop and ordered a chocolate cupcake with light blue swirl frosting and a small cappuccino. After her incident with Siobhan, Edith swore to keep her coffee orders simple. The cashier was a pale brunette man with familiar turquoise eyes. Edith looked to the side, tapping into her thoughts while waiting for her order at the bar.

Her phone vibrated in her pocket.

You can have me in about twenty minutes.

Edith grinned at her husband's text.

I'll be at Swan Café & Bakery. It's the little shop down the street.

Of course, you've grown tired of Radley's Espresso. I'm kidding, by the way.

See you soon, Mr. Radley.

Edith twisted the rings on her finger and held her hand up to admire them. A woman next to stared from the corner of her eye. Edith looked back at her and parted her lips, noticing the bakery line getting longer.

She made eye contact with the cashier, who flashed a nervous smile and chuckled.

"I'll be right there, Miss. Just give me one second." he patted his hands on his apron and walked over to the espresso machine.

He gave Edith a double take, but the decor of the establishment distracted her. There were white marble floors, gray and blue patterned walls, large windows, and a glass door. Paintings on the wall contrasted the pastel shades with their bold, dark tones.

"Admiring the place, huh?" he smiles. Edith's stomach squeezed.

"It's nice. I love the decor and colors." she smiles halfway.

"Thanks," he says. A customer in line groans. "Here is your cappuccino, and I hope you enjoy your cupcake," he shuffled back to the register and listened to the frowning man complain about desperately needing his vanilla latte.

"Thank you,"

Edith gave another faint smile, shoved the phone back into her pocket to hold the items, and seated herself at a tall table. She sipped the coffee, making a tiny slurp.

Two employees walked in from the backroom.

"Hey, Noah. I'm sorry we took so long."

The woman tied the apron around her waist and walked over to the coffee machines. The other patted Noah on the back.

"I can take it from here,"

Her perfume mixed with cigarettes gave the bakery a unique aroma. Impatient customers sucked in their breaths. Some covered their noses with scarves or the neck of their shirts.

"I know, I get it," the replacement groaned. "What can I do for you?"

Noah stepped out from behind the counter and walked over to Edith, glancing at his watch for the time. *Felix is taking longer than twenty minutes. Edith chugged her coffee slowly.*

"Edith, right?" Noah asks.

"Um, yeah. I'm Edith. Do I know you?" She looked around and at the door.

"It's me, Noah. We met in college?"

He glanced at her hand. She smiles, raising her hand up to her face subconsciously. The diamonds shimmered.

"Oh! Noah. Noah Sullivan?"

Noah was one of Edith's classmates during her third year at UMass Boston. Getting a bachelor's degree felt so long ago. She couldn't remember which subject they had together and stared at her cup. She looked into Noah's eyes.

"Right." his eyes twinkled. The smile never left. "So, how've you been, Edith?"

"I've been well, just trying to get by in life. I've recently transferred to a new job. Is this your bakery?" Her thoughts shifted in a minute.

"Yeah, this is my bakery. I signed the lease a month ago. As you can see, business is booming for now," he looked over at the staff. "Where do you work, Edith?" Felix entered, fixing the sleeve of his suit jacket. This is why I hate suit jackets; he thought. He darted his eyes at the love of his life, smiling and then lowered his eyes at the man sitting with her.

"Hi, babe,"

He stepped over and gave Edith a peck on the cheek. Felix looked behind him to see people in line gawking at him. He politely waved at the poor staff handling disgruntled customers. Edith finished a bite of her cupcake.

"Hold on," a slight English twang slid on Noah's tongue. "You're Radley, aren't you?" he stood up from the seat, gazing at the man. "Felix Radley! Oh, my god!"

"It's always a pleasure meeting a fan," Felix lowered his temper, giving Noah a welcoming grin. Noah held out his hand for a shake. Mr. Radley accepted it.

"This is amazing! Edith, you're married to the top tech CEO of the state!"

"Well, I wouldn't say I'm at the top…"

Noah pulled out a pad and pen from his apron as if he'd been dying for this moment. Edith rested on her hand, watching the scene occur.

"Can I have your autograph? My name's Noah," Felix gestured for Edith to get up.

"Sure, why not?" he wrote To Noah, and scribbled his name. Before a stampede could ensue, Felix grabbed Edith's hand. "Here you go," he says, returning the pad and pen. He gave Noah another smile before hauling his wife out of the bakery.

She looked back at the adoring fan.

"It was nice to see you, Noah."

Once home, Felix held the door for Edith as she stepped inside. She reached for the remote and turned on the fireplace. He sat on the loveseat, gesturing for her to sit with him.

"Who was that guy at the bakery?"

He peeled his suit jacket off and laid it on the back pillow. Edith laid back, resting her head on his lap. "That was Noah. He was an old classmate,"

"Okay." he tugged at her hair and twirled a strand around his finger playfully. "What college did you go to? I never asked."

"I went to UMass Boston and Stanford."

Felix raised his eyebrows and let go of her hair, resting his arm. "That's interesting, why Stanford?"

She sat up and pulled down her blouse.

"Everyone I knew in high school went to UC Berkeley." she chuckled dryly.

Edith propped her knees up, moving just a little to give Felix space. "What school did you attend, Mr. Top CEO?" she grinned.

"I attended UC Berkeley."

Edith dropped her jaw, sweating on the side of her face.

"Really?"

"No," he laughed. "I also went to Stanford."

Edith stared at her toes.

We would've crossed each other's paths.

"It's nice to visit California and study there, but Massachusetts is still my home."

She looked up at Felix, curving her lips.

"Mine too,"

Felix leaned in for her lips, but his phone's loud ringtone pulled him back.

"Hi, Gertrude. Yes, okay." he stood up and searched in between the seat cushions for his keys. Edith pointed at the coffee table. "I'll be there to pick him up," Felix hung up the phone and gave Edith a swift kiss, then swiped his keys off the table. "I'm going to pick up Grayson," he tells her.

Felix left his suit jacket and slipped on his shoes. Edith closed the door as her husband walked to his car.

Edith went to the office to check on her emails. There was a box with white wrapping and a blue ribbon sitting on the office chair. She pulled a card from underneath the ribbon.

As your wedding gift.

I know sharing my laptop can be a hassle.

xo Felix

Felix returned with Grayson in his arms. In a few months, Grayson will be a year old and they'd have to worry about him crawling around.

Edith put the card down.

"I'm in here," Felix grinned from ear to ear.

"Did you see your gift?" he looked at the box.

"Open it,"

Edith untied the ribbon. She ran her fingers over the edges of the box and ripped the wrapper off immediately. It was the latest model of a Dell XPS laptop. She looked over at her husband and went over to hug him. Her arm wrapped around Grayson, hugging him, too. Edith reached her face up to Felix's for a thank you kiss.

"I'm a busy man and you're a busy woman, so you shouldn't have to worry about getting work finished on time,"

"My boss would want me to finish work on time."

"Your efforts mesmerized your boss,"

"Oh?"

"I have my love language and you have yours. I'll be right back." he turned to the door and walked out, leaving Edith staring at the box again.

While she waited for him to put the baby in his crib, Edith took the laptop out of its box, noting its new tech smell, something that was highly familiar to her since working at Brighton. Felix returned to the office just as she placed her Dell on the desk next to his MacBook Pro. She didn't mind the difference in price or operating systems.

He placed her hands on his waist. "I'd do anything to keep you happy," he kissed up her neck and planted his lips on hers.

"Are we doing it here?" she breathed. Edith gripped onto the edge of the desk. It vibrated from her weight.

"Do you want to?" his lips burned through her skin. The right side of her neck was his favorite spot to peck.

"Let's take this somewhere else,"

Her moan prompted Felix to lift her up and tangle her legs around his waist. She wrapped her arms around his neck as he carried her to the living room.

Edith's toes curled as Felix finished inside her. They laid with their backs on the rug and throw blanket at the waist. Edith stared at the ceiling. "I can't believe we just did that on an ancient rug."

Felix turned his head. "Ancient rug?"

She let out a brief laugh.

"My parents bought it in Romania years back. They gave it to me as a gift when they came to Massachusetts years ago."

Felix raised his eyebrows.

"Huh,"

"I clean it periodically so don't sweat it," she laughs.

"Do you miss your parents?"

He turned on his side and grabbed the pillow next to him, tucking it under his head.

"Sometimes I think about visiting them."

They looked into each other's eyes.

"When do you want to see them?"

"What?" she sat up, holding the blanket to her chest. Edith's cheeks turned pink.

Felix sat up, facing her.

"If you could see them again, when would you want to?" he stared at the rug for a second. "I'd like to meet your parents one day. It doesn't have to be straight away. I just think it's the right thing to do."

The pit of Edith's stomach twisted into a knot. She hadn't spoken to her parents about having a partner, let alone a child. They were kind about her studying and having a growing career, but her love life wasn't something she would feel comfortable disclosing.

"Felix, they don't know that I'm dating anyone, let alone married to anyone," she stammered. Felix looked at her, concerned. "I haven't told them because we have many customs and traditions. You and I, you know, started as a hookup. Remember?"

"Edith," he exhaled. "I wanted to keep things quiet in the office, but I had expected you to say one thing to your parents about me. It doesn't have to be about our sex life." "What about Grayson?"

"They'd probably love Grayson."

Edith bit her lip. She had a coded string of possibilities projecting in her mind.

"You're my boss,"

"They might find that impressive. You'll never know," he smirked.

"What if…"

Felix placed his hands on her shoulders, looking Edith straight in the eyes.

"No more what ifs," he licked his lips. "Telling your parents about us is better than keeping it a secret."

"Okay,"

29

It rained heavily in Boston. The chill air showed that snow was on its way. Last December, Edith and Felix didn't think about celebrating Christmas. There were no presents. They sat on the loveseat and warmed up in front of the fireplace. They spent half the day on binge-watching movies.

This time, Felix wanted to do something different. She knew of his family and the family business. It humbled him to inquire about her own. Edith stared at the photo of her parents in her hand. *It was painful to be away, but I love being alone. Will they be happy to see me?* They visited her when she settled into Brighton Technologies. Back when she was only in IT. People in Edith's hometown thought a bright young woman her age was promising. Her parents moved from Moldavia to Bucharest.

While the Radleys owned a private jet, it was family owned and dear to his grandfather's heart. Felix opted to buy First Class plane tickets. Edith looked into Felix's suitcase. She laughed and he raised his eyebrows.

"Are you Mr. Casual on vacation? Where are the suits and ties?" She bit her lip, amused.

Felix stroked Edith's hair and kissed the side of her head.

"I don't want anyone to think I'm part of the CIA or something, and I enjoy dressing like a regular guy. Just not in the office,"

"At home, you're Mr. Plaid Pajamas." she continued grinning. Felix dropped his eyes to the neatly folded t-shirts and jeans.

"Should I unpack then?"

Edith touched his chin and kissed his lips.

"I like this casual side of you,"

"Yeah?" his eyes lit back up.

"All parts of my husband are sexy,"

"Mmm," he wrapped his arm around her waist, pulling her in for a sensual, energetic kiss. Felix nearly glued his lips to hers. "We should hurry if you don't want to be late. I just wanted to double check everything."

"Of course," she says, while tossing the hairbrush into her purse.

Coming from North End, they didn't have to drive too far. Their flight was in two hours. People came from entrances left and right. Wheels rolled and skidded across the floor. Some travelers yelled and cried; afraid they wouldn't get on a plane on time. Felix held Edith's hand as they walked to the check-in line. An old woman was kind enough to have them cut in line.

Standing, waiting, listening to everyone boast about how they booked months ahead for the trip of the year actually helped kill time. When they made it on the airplane, Felix shoved Edith's carry-on into the compartment above their seats.

He sat down and kissed the back of her hand, holding it close.

"What do you think they'll say to me? To us?" her eyes blurred as she spoke.

"I can imagine they'd welcome us with open arms. Do you know if other relatives will be there?"

"Not a clue," she sighed.

"Edith," he tilted her chin and kissed her deeply. "Enough sighing."

The estimated time was sixteen hours. This was shorter than both their work hours combined on a good day.

"Would you rather sit in your office for sixteen hours or be on the recliner for sixteen hours?" Edith chuckled.

"Recliner. I will always choose my recliner." he looked into her tired eyes. Wrinkles formed at the corners. "I'm curious. Do you speak Romanian?"

Edith shrugged.

"I must have when I was a child, but I don't remember any words now. Don't worry, my parents speak English,"

"Just saying, I would've found you a hundred times more attractive if you were bilingual," he laughed, choking on spit.

He patted Edith's arm.

"You're quite the comedian, Mr. Radley," she whispered and yawned. Edith rested her head on his shoulder before shutting her eyes.

The flight attendant handed Felix a blanket, as requested. He spread the blanket across Edith and himself. Buzzing from the air pressure and plane engine caused Felix's right ear to ring. At least Edith sat by the window. He closed his own eyes and drifted to sleep.

"Felix, honey," his mother's voice called. "Please call your sister. Dinner is ready in a minute."

Twelve-year-old Felix ran upstairs and knocked on Lola's door.

"Mom says the food's ready," his scratchy deepening voice cracked. He listened for a reply.

"When is dad coming home?"

"He'll be late,"

"I won't eat until dad's there."

Felix sighed. Even then, he didn't like to push people. He ran down the stairs to report to his mom. She sat at the table alone, picking at the peas on her plate.

"Is your sister coming?"

Felix shrugged.

"She said she won't eat until dad is here,"

Eliana looked at her son and stood up from the table. "You can eat, then." she says. "Lola!" She walked up the stairs and Felix pulled his chair out, grimacing at the peas and poking at the well-done steak on his plate.

The couple slept through their dinner hour. Felix groaned, opening his eyes. He must have been hungry.

"That was a strange dream." he muttered. Or was it a memory?

Staring out the window at the pitch-black sky and gray clouds made Felix feel cold, as if he was outside flying through the wind. He listened to Edith breathe and observed the side of her face. *She looks so peaceful.*

Edith murmured and clutched onto the blanket.

He grabbed the headphones in front of him and tapped on the screen for something to watch. Felix spends more of his time reviewing proposals and facilitating people. He rarely had time for movies and books. Sometimes, he would finish reading an online article or two.

The movie *Click* starring Adam Sandler was a random choice he made. I've seen this movie a long time ago. He adjusted himself and sat comfortably. *Champagne sounds good right now.*

Felix held a finger up, getting the flight attendant's attention.

"Is there something you need, sir?" her voice was soft. Felix couldn't help but stare at her voluptuous figure.

"Could I get champagne and two ibuprofens, please? Thank you,"

"Of course, sir." she says.

His mind drifted, watching the woman walk away. Felix exhaled and continued to look for another movie to watch. Within minutes, the attendant came back with his request, giving Felix a quick wink and a smile before moving on to the next person.

You don't know how much power you truly have, Felix.

He scoffed at the thought.

When the airplane was close to landing, the pilot announced a one-hour warning. Edith lifted her head and squinted. "We're here already?" she asked.

"We'll be approaching Bucharest soon."

The driver picked Edith and Felix up from the airport, taking them to her parents' home address. Edith kept the post-it with their phone number scribbled onto it. She dialed the phone number and her mama answered. "Mama, I'm almost home. I brought a guest with me," she smiles. Felix looked away from the window mouthing, *a guest?*

"You're almost here?" Alina exclaimed. "I don't believe it! Mihai! Edith is almost home!" she nearly sobbed into the phone.

"I will see you and Tata soon," Edith sniffled. "Yes, I'll be safe. I love you. Bye for now,"

Edith lowered the phone in shock. A tear streamed down from her right eye. Felix pressed his hand against her cheek, wiping her tears away.

"My mother seemed overjoyed. They want to see me… to see us." she held her breath and exhaled. Her cheeks turned pale again.

<h1 style="text-align:center">30</h1>

Clouds gathered in the sky. Felix rubbed his hands together to warm up.

"Someone's getting cold now, shall we head back?" Edith smirked.

Felix nodded and grabbed her hand.

"This makes me feel a little better."

They walked back, trudging in the snow. Edith held onto Felix's arm. The streets soon filled with laughter and conversations as they passed people by. A little girl smiles and waved at the two while she drew on the snow with a stick.

When they got back to the house, Edith's father was sitting at the table and her mother lit up the fireplace.

"Welcome back," Alina says. "How was your walk?" she entered the kitchen and poured liquid into mugs. She walked over to them, smiling. "I made some Filtru or brewed coffee,"

Edith and Felix sat on the side of the table. Mihai was sitting at the end. He looked up from the book he was reading and looked over at Felix who slowly sipped his coffee.

"Felix, if I may ask. How old are you? You look quite young," Mihai asked.

Felix smiles briefly.

He felt heat in his cheeks rise, unsure if it was from the drink. "I'm thirty-four, sir."

"Oh, really? Interesting, and where are you from?" Mihai scooted his chair in and closed his book. Felix exhaled but forced a smile. His hands steamed. "My father is from England and my mother is from South America. I was born and raised in Boston… sir."

"South America? How grand!" Alina placed her hands on top of the chair, listening to their conversation. "Where in South America?"

"Argentina,"

Alina's ears perked and she raised her eyebrows. "Wonderful, I can see that in your complexion," she laughs.

Edith stared into her mug, not expecting her parents to interview her husband on his vacation. *What's next? Please don't suggest a Romanian wedding. We don't need another wedding.* Edith bit down on her lip and smiles nervously. Alina looked at her daughter and sat across from Felix, smiling from ear to ear. The wrinkles formed in the corners of her eyes. Edith drank her coffee halfway.

"What's your grandfather like? I hear about him on the news. He used to make speeches on screen."

"Ah yes, Louis, was it?"

"Do you have siblings, dear?"

Edith's eyes began to dry. Felix brushed his foot against hers. Edith cleared her throat, splitting the noise.

"Please excuse me," she stood up without looking at them and pushed in her chair.

Felix got up with her. "Excuse us,"

She turned, heading to the bedroom. Felix rubbed the middle of her back and closed the door behind them. She removed her coat and sat on the bed. Regardless of wearing leggings, her dress rose up. Felix sat next to her, and pushed her hair back.

"Is something wrong?"

Edith's heart palpitated, even more with Felix's hand on her knee.

"This is what they do…" she sniffled. "My parents will bombard someone with questions until they'd walk away from me… run from me." She tucked hair behind her ear. Felix breathed out a laugh.

"People ask me a thousand questions a day. I can handle it," he lowered his voice.

"You're not bothered by my dad's personal questions?" She wiped the eyelash that fell on her cheek.

Felix shook his head and pressed his lips together. "I was a tiny bit uncomfortable but I understand where he's coming from. It's rare for people to talk to big bosses and personal lives genuinely intrigue people."

"They're not just anyone. They're family."

Felix kissed her softly, tasting the salt from her tears. "And you're my family now… which includes them." he sighed, putting his arm around her shoulder. "If you don't want to stay, we can go elsewhere. We could tour other parts of Romania or since we're in Europe, I'll take you anywhere you want to go,"

"Can we?"

"Name a place. You're in my life now, Edith. Life should be celebrated and there's so little time. I'm not running away from you; I'm running with you. So, let's just go,"

31

Instead of a one-week stay as planned, the two packed up and booked for France. This was a perk Edith didn't think she would have, marrying a tech tycoon. The five-hour flight would have been like flying from Seattle to Los Angeles. On the plane, Edith thought about how easy Felix's childhood must have been when his parents were around.

"Felix,"

"Hmm?" His eyes moved all around the pamphlet that he took. There were plenty of things to do in France.

"Do you remember your parents? What were they like?" she tapped her chin. "What about your sister?" Felix lowered the pamphlet from his eyes. He closed it and put it down on the tray in front of him.

"There are a few things I remember," his voice cracked. "Like going carnivals and I used to walk my sister to school…" he trailed.

He swallowed, trying not to unlock the sensitive memory. Edith took his hand. She wanted to focus on him instead.

"What were you like as a child?" Felix took a breath. "I was into sports. I played soccer and almost tried out for football in high school."

The corner of Edith's mouth curved up.

"What changed?" "No one would attend the games, so I quit early." Edith saw the twinkle fade from his eyes. *Oh, you poor thing.*

"Edith, I know you're curious about me, but I haven't thought about the past in years. I'd like to keep it that way." he touched her cheek.

"Okay,"

"Ask anything I can talk about." He brushed his lips against her cheeks, leaving a mark and pulling away. "From now on, you and I are both moving forward."

When they landed in Paris, it was smooth sailing from there. It looked beautiful this time of year. Plenty of visitors crowded in front of the Eiffel Tower. The couple hailed a cab and Edith looked out the window, pointing at things she found interesting. Felix kept his eyes on her with his heart pounding.

They booked a room at Le Meurice and toured for the rest of the day. They visited the Louvre and kissed in front of the Palace of Versailles. He lifted her up and spun her around like what they'd do in movies. Edith's heel slipped off and fell to the ground, causing locals to give them looks.

It felt like they were doing everything backwards, going on dates and meeting the parents post marriage, and even having a child before saying 'I do'. Maybe that's the secret to strengthening their bond. Edith felt like their relationship was passing by at the speed of light, but like Felix said, life was getting shorter.

No one in Paris treated Felix like a celebrity. He was sure there were foreign investors from France. Brighton Tech was a mega hit in Europe. However, the lack of screaming fans made him feel like a normal person for once.

While exploring the streets of Paris, they passed by a shop window. Edith stared at the silk slip dress at the window and wanted to inquire about it. They stepped inside and she immediately looked at the tag.

"Felix," she says, not risking to leave a fingerprint on the precious garment. "It's four-hundred dollars."

"You know how much I love silk." he says. Felix leaned into Edith's ear and whispered, "Consider it your Christmas present," she blushed at his comment and he turned to the salesperson. "We'll take that one, please." He made the transaction, and they walked out of the store with two dresses in different colors. Felix kissed her temple. "You'll be wearing one of them tonight for me." Edith knew where this would lead. They continued to walk around. Felix ignored the rising pain in his calves. *I can walk upstairs but I can't walk around Paris?* He scoffed. They stopped, and hauled a cab back to the hotel.

The sky dimmed in a timely manner.

When they arrived at the hotel and entered the room, Edith threw herself onto the bed and hugged the pillow, feeling the soft cotton against her cheeks. Felix turned off the lights and switched the lamps on.

He pulled her slip dress out of the bag.

"Are you forgetting something?" he held up the dress, and she started to peel off her top. "Allow me,"

Edith put her arms down. Felix checked the door, then laid her cream silk dress on the bed gently and pulled Edith's shirt up above her head. He tugged at the button of her jeans and zipped it down with one hard pull. She watched as he tossed her clothes onto the floor and snapped her bra off. He peeled her thong and tossed it into the messy pile.

"When did you first like silk?"

Her question made him chuckle.

"I'm a man of many tastes."

Honestly, I don't remember.

He slipped the dress over her head and pulled it down, moving one hand up her inner thigh.

She groaned from his warm palm.

Felix wrapped an arm around Edith, carrying her weight, and laid her on the bed. Her head was in between the two pillows. He hovered over her like many times before. There wasn't lust in his eyes, but pure admiration. Edith felt slippery in her silk dress.

The man stripped his shirt off and stepped out of his jeans. Edith's eyes widened at his hard-on.

He lifted the dress and rose above her hip, palming her right side. Her skin was slightly cold to the touch. "This will be the honeymoon you wanted, Edith."

She swallowed and looked into the pools of his eyes. He crawled on top, making their eyes meet. She's seen his inner beast give her a cue to make a choice before. She would have run or let her guard down. This moment made Edith reach her right hand down to her front. The space between them let her, but he didn't. Felix swiftly grabbed her hand and locked his fingers in between hers.

He held the naughty hand above her head, slightly pressuring her palm. Edith gasped. Her other arm surrendered.

"We'll be taking this nice and slow, my love." he whispered in a husky tone.

One wrong move and he won't take it slow. Felix's ideas of lovemaking were easy to distinguish.

When he's hungry and the lion wants to pounce, he'll use his force and reckless power to take what he wants. Edith once was a cautious colleague, completely unaware of this animal. Now, he's tamed. There was no reason for the lion to attack unless he felt it was necessary. He can also be delicate and sensual. He can make Edith beg for it.

"Felix," she swallowed.

"Mmm," he traced her hardening nipple through the silk. "Be a good girl for me." he released her hand and pinched her right nipple.

Felix kissed her softly. He won't be her dominant tonight. Edith sank into the pillows further, allowing her senses to go along with him. He wanted to take things slowly. Fuck taking it slow, his mind barked. Keeping his lips on hers, Felix moved to slip his boxers off. He opened one eye and tossed the shorts on the floor. Holding the cock in his hand, Edith's pussy sensed what would happen. She spread her legs.

She wrapped her arms around and dug her nails into his back, feeling him go in deeper with the beginning thrusts. "You feel good, don't you?" His words sent waves of ecstasy through her. Her mind spun in circles with each impeding thrust.

"Make me cum, Felix," she breathed.

He pulled out and thrusted hard, repeating the motion as she moaned into his mouth.

"More?" he smirks.

He watched her mouth open and close while he picked up the pace. Edith's eyes slightly roll back as she focused on achieving a climax. The ripples inside her couldn't stay. He rose and held her by the hips. Edith bucked her hips as his cock slid freely. "Mmmm, fuck me, Mr. Radley!"

Felix leaned to kiss her. "Are you calling me Mr. Radley outside of the office now?" he chuckled.

Edith opened her eyes, thinking he would stop. Felix bit his bottom lip and smiles. Calling him Mr. Radley only made his cock pulse. He pumped slowly, then forced himself to go faster.

"Oh, shit! Yes, please!"

Her tone was melodic to him. Edith continued to squeal and moan. She panted, feeling herself unleash. He gripped onto her hips and pumped harder, quicker. He worked her for another ten minutes before releasing into her.

They cleaned themselves up in the bathroom, and Edith washed her hands a second time. Felix stood behind Edith and kissed her neck. She smiles and looks into his eyes.

"It's almost Christmas. How long are we going to be in Europe for?" "We can stay here until New Year's." he groaned, kissing down her neck.

"Felix," she turned and touched his chest. "We have a child, remember?"

"Shit," he laughed. "We can have two more nights in Paris, then we can leave."

Half his lips wanted to frown.

Edith will have to spend more time away from Grayson and then it's back to work. Felix sighed. Nothing lasts forever, and a vacation is temporary. He wrapped his arms around her before stepping to the sink. She returned to the bed and sat on the edge, scrolling on her phone.

A text message from Albert pinged on her phone.

Edith scrunched her nose. *When did I give Albert my phone number?* He sent a photo of a dark-haired man in a suit and a blonde in a wedding dress. She was in his arms, lifted from the ground.

Edith swiped her thumbs on the phone. Albert, how did you… She blinked at the three dots on the screen. *Good morning, Edith,* he typed. I *wanted to let you know. Bianca and the Vice President got married. They invited me to their wedding today.* Edith backspaced, erasing her text.

"Bianca and the VP?" she whispered. She held the phone closer to her face. Edith chuckled, astonished.

Felix turned the bathroom light off and shut the door behind him. "What's up?" he looked at the screen when she turned the phone to face him. "Bianca and Kyle? They're hitched?"

Both Edith and Felix laughed.

Edith laid back down on the bed. "Well, the office never knew about us, but these two will be the talk of the town now."

"I'd rather have people talking about them than about us, and that's none of our concern now."

"You're still the CEO," Felix groaned and sat down next to her. "You're right. I'll probably hear about this in the morning."

There was a delay going from France to Boston. The forecast reported a storm brewing. When they landed in Boston, the lands were dry and frost highlighted the sidewalks.

Felix left their suitcases and coats in the living room. "I'll be back soon," he says, kissing Edith's cheek. His bottom lip barely reached her jawline. "Stay out of trouble," he lightly giggled and shut the door.

Not once had Edith come to pick Grayson up because Felix enjoyed the minutes spent in the car with him. Despite their 'no gossip' rule, Edith was itching to know the state of Bianca's reputation. Albert was still good friends with either of them and was doing his part of filling Edith in with Brighton Tech activities.

Edith sat in the recliner and rubbed her calves. She glanced at her suitcase, wanting to unpack, but removing things was a lot harder than folding and inserting items into her suitcases.

She pushed the recliner back and turned the TV on. House hunting wasn't particularly on her mind, but the reality show clarified that it was time to think about it. It won't be long before Grayson turned a year old. She scanned the room, remembering when she bought the house at twenty-three years old.

Edith chuckled.

That was when Max was a newly divorced man. Everyone groaned at the idea of a young woman purchasing her first house straight out of college. Max thought she was brilliant and ahead for someone her age. She thought about how Max would mow his front lawn every Saturday morning and glance across the street once in a while, hoping Edith would come outside to talk to him.

She was always in the living room reviewing files to send to the directors.

Edith would take reports home and critique them as if she were a college professor. She was that dedicated to her job as an engineering manager back then. Edith's phone vibrated on the coffee table.

There's traffic, I'll be home in half an hour.

Edith stood with a hand on her hip and pursed her lips, looking at the suitcases. *I guess I should put things away now.*

Okay, be safe. I love you.

Felix typed back.

I love you too.

Edith spent time cleaning up. She lugged the suitcases into the bedroom closet. She hung the tops and bottoms, then threw the worn clothes into the washer. She stared at the other silk slip dress.

"Time for a shower,"

She removed her clothes and hopped into the shower, adjusting the knob for warm temperature. Edith rinsed her hair, pulling it back. She closed her eyes and let the steam massage the pores on her face.

Minutes passed. The bathroom door opened and Felix walked in, shirtless. He pulled on the shower door and joined in. Stepping behind her, Felix rested his chin on her shoulder.

"So, you want to wear the other lingerie?"

Edith felt his amusement.

She nodded. "Did you check on Grayson before you stripped?" she massaged shampoo into her hair.

Felix pulled her into him.

He breathed. "Yes, he's asleep," he pressed his lips onto hers, following one kiss after another. "Edith," he moaned. "Play with me,"

"What?" she moaned, shutting her eyes.

Her shampoo washed away. She turned around and led her hands up to his hair. Felix whispered into her ear.

"I missed my little minx." Her toes curled at the word.

"I missed you, Mr. Radley,"

ABOUT
NORA S. PATTUGALAN

NORA S. PATTUGALAN is a Romance author and fiction writer residing in Washington. She has published online articles and two novels. Her work can be found on norapauthor.com. Nora grew up in Seattle, WA developing a passion for the Humanities subject. Since her sophomore year of high school, she has read a variety of romance novels and began writing her first stories during college.

Nora has a Bachelor's Degree in Humanities with Minors in English and Psychology.

Integrating philosophy and psychology, the author weaves the topic of love in each story to drive discussion and curiosity. She loves stories that thrill.